✍ Baying and rushing, a pack of dogs skittered down the trail.

Dad didn't look back. He sent his Appaloosa surging forward, jumping ahead to level footing. Then, Dad turned Jeep to face the dogs.

Sam couldn't tell how many there were. Four? Maybe five?

Dad had Jeep under control, but the Appaloosa was scared.

Dogs were predators.

Horses were prey.

Dad lifted his coiled rope. In a backhand smack, he struck at the biggest dog, but not before it nipped the Appaloosa's nose.

It was too much.

Jeep was stronger than Dad was heavy. He soared into a full rear, nose dripping blood. When the speckled hound leapt a second time, as if going for the horse's throat, Jeep tried to stand even taller. He fell. ⌒

Read all the books about the

Phantom Stallion

Phantom Stallion

❧ 14 ❧
Moonrise

TERRI FARLEY

AVON BOOKS

An Imprint of HarperCollins*Publishers*

Library of Congress Catalog Card Number:
2004095685
ISBN 0-06-058315-0

First Avon edition, 2005

AVON TRADEMARK REG. U.S. PAT. OFF. AND IN OTHER COUNTRIES,
MARCA REGISTRADA, HECHO EN U.S.A.

❖

Visit us on the World Wide Web!
www.harperchildrens.com

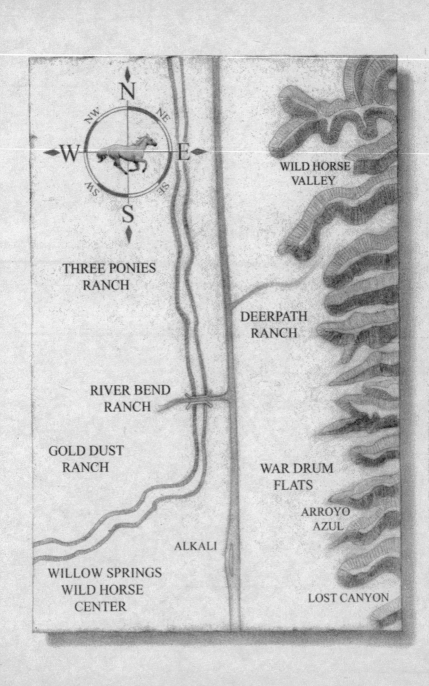

Chapter One ∞

Mustangs weren't supposed to pout.

They didn't brood over unfairness or store up bad days in their equine minds until they spotted a chance to pay someone back.

It just wasn't the sort of thing mustangs did, but no one had told Ace.

"You're not a sea horse," Samantha Forster told her bay gelding. "We can't stay out here in the lake. If someone comes riding along and spots us, it will be really embarrassing."

Once, Ace had been a wild mustang whose black mane and tail flew back from his red-gold coat as he galloped across the range, but he sure wasn't running now.

Moonrise 1

Instead, Ace stood in the middle of the shallow lake on War Drum Flats. He stared toward the horizon where the white desert floor met the broad blue Nevada sky.

He splashed one hoof in the water. The droplets felt cool as they soaked through Sam's jeans, but any experienced rider would agree with her: She couldn't let her mount get away with this.

"Come on, Ace. Jen will be here any minute." Sam sat straighter in her saddle. She used her legs, heels, and hands to urge her horse forward. Again.

Her best friend, Jennifer Kenworthy, was supposed to meet her here at ten o'clock.

Sam glanced at her watch. Jen was almost always on time. That meant Sam had eight minutes to convince her horse he belonged ashore. The only reason there was no audience for Ace's stunt was because they'd arrived early.

There was almost no audience. That squawk from a blue jay gliding overhead sounded a lot like laughter.

Sam blamed herself for trusting Ace. She knew he had a mischievous nature, especially when he hadn't been worked enough.

After a lope across the range, she'd allowed Ace a long drink at the lake while she thought about the overnight campout she and Jen were planning.

If she'd been paying attention, Ace might not

have fooled her into believing he was just wading out for a drink. He'd gone a few steps farther than she'd expected. And then a few more. Her first clue that the tricky bay was headed for the middle of the shallow lake had come when he'd given such a lunge that water spattered her stirrups.

Just as she'd tried to turn Ace, his hooves had lifted, and she'd experienced the uncanny feeling of riding a swimming horse. Excitement and worry had played tug-of-war in her brain, as Ace's legs surged and pulled and she floated along with him.

Finally, he'd settled his hooves so that he stood chest-deep in muddy water. Only by holding her boot toes up was she keeping her polished leather stirrups clear of the muck he'd stirred from the lake bottom.

He'd ignored her instructions since then. Because orders weren't working, Sam tried bribery.

She rubbed Ace's favorite spot at the base of his mane. "Doesn't that feel good, boy?" she said. "As soon as we get back to shore I'll do it some more."

Too smart for bribery, Ace twitched his skin as if she were a fly.

Next, Sam tried peer pressure.

"Let's go, boy. I think Silly will laugh at you."

Silk Stockings was Jen's palomino mare. Jen called her horse Silly, and claimed she only rode the mare to study horse neuroses for her future career as a veterinarian.

Sam could imagine Silly jigging and pulling at her reins trying to swim after Ace, but she couldn't imagine *Jen* giving her mount enough rein to pull the stunt Ace had.

All at once, Ace tensed beneath her.

An eerie howl raised chills on Sam's arms in spite of the summer warmth.

Lost Canyon wasn't too far away. It was supposed to be haunted, but she didn't believe that.

"Coyotes?" Sam asked Ace.

The gelding's ears pointed toward the mountains. He answered with an inquiring snort.

Coyotes howled at night, singing before a hunt and yapping their excitement afterward. Sam heard them almost every night and she knew what they sounded like. These howls were different.

Then she saw dust swirling on one of the mountain paths.

"Are those horses?" she asked Ace.

Wild horses rarely ran during midmorning, but if they had a reason—could coyotes be stalking the Phantom's newborn foals?

Sam's heart thudded crazily.

Mustangs were born to run. If they outdistanced their pursuers right away, the foals would be fine. For a time, they'd keep up with the herd as it fled, but those delicate legs had to take two running strides to match each of their mothers'.

Sam wished she had binoculars. She wanted to

see what was going on, but it was just too far away.

If the mustangs had been coming down to water, wouldn't they keep running this way?

"Come out here," she urged the horses. "You're safer in the open."

Sam dropped her reins. Ace wasn't going anywhere, anyway, and she'd read once that you could improve your vision slightly and temporarily by pulling the corners of your eyes.

She tried it. It helped a little bit, sharpening her view of faraway horses that were crashing through thickets of sagebrush. It didn't look like many horses. They might even have riders. And she still couldn't see what was after them.

Sam groaned in frustration. Even if Ace moved, would it help to go galloping up that hillside into the midst of an attack?

Ace shifted nervously, so Sam took up her reins again.

"Why don't they come down here?" Sam asked.

Horses had a better chance of kicking and biting their attackers, instead of each other, if they weren't crowded together like they were in that steep, brushy ravine.

If *she* knew that, the Phantom had to, as well.

"It can't be him," Sam told Ace.

Even though he was young for a herd stallion, the Phantom was experienced. The fleet silver mustang had protected his band for at least two years. He wouldn't allow his foals to be cornered and struck down by predators.

An angry neigh shrilled down from the hillside and Sam caught a flash of blue-black hide.

"Oh my gosh," Sam gasped.

New Moon. Of course there were other black mustangs on this range, but it could be him.

Last summer, the Phantom had been captured and forced to buck in a rodeo. In his absence, New Moon, the Phantom's son, had tried to take over.

His reign hadn't lasted long. Once the Phantom had returned, he'd driven New Moon away from the family herd. In the fall, the young black stallion had challenged his father and lost. Sam hadn't seen him since.

Now, Sam struggled for a better view, but there was nothing to see.

Just as suddenly as it had begun, the commotion ended. No manes showed above the thicket. Dust drifted on the morning breeze, spinning into threads, thinning, then disappearing.

Sam listened intently. She heard no possessive yaps from coyotes with a meal to protect and no yelps from subordinate coyotes being driven away from a kill. Sam closed her eyes to concentrate, but all she heard was tires, as a vehicle passed on the highway, beyond the lake and over the ridge.

Suddenly, she heard a voice.

". . . you doing?"

It was Jen.

Sam waved. She'd been so focused on the horses, she hadn't seen Jen ride up to the edge of the lake.

"Ace won't move!" Sam shouted back. She was eager to tell Jen what she'd seen, but right now she had to get Ace out of the water.

Jen shook her head. Her white-blond braids flipped around her shoulders and sunlight glinted on the lenses of her glasses. Then she pointed to one ear.

She hadn't heard.

"He's getting back at me for neglecting him!" Sam bellowed this time.

Jen seemed to hear, but not agree. She tossed a braid back over the shoulder of her magenta blouse.

"You're giving him more credit—or blame—than he deserves," Jen called.

Sam shrugged. Jen teased her for attributing human emotions to horses. But Sam had spent two weeks paying more attention to her new filly, Tempest, and to Jinx, a bucking horse in need of a second chance, than to Ace. Why *wouldn't* Ace show his jealousy?

Jen rode Silly a few steps into the lake. Now that she was closer, she didn't have to yell.

"If I were any kind of a roper, I'd try to rope him and lead him out," Jen offered.

Sam shook her head.

"That'd just make him mad," she said. "I could get off and lead him."

Sam looked down. Her legs were trembling from holding her boot toes up to keep them, and her stirrups, out of the water.

If she climbed off, she'd be soaked. Remounting—she sure wasn't going to *walk* home—would make her saddle so filthy that she'd have to spend all afternoon cleaning it.

"Wait," Jen said, looking away. She shielded the lenses of her glasses from the sun's glare. "Someone's coming."

"My dad," Sam said, though she only hoped it was. Actually, she'd settle for Jen's dad, or Dallas, the foreman of River Bend Ranch. She'd rather it wasn't Pepper, their youngest cowboy. It was pretty embarrassing to be stuck in the middle of a lake because your own horse was ignoring you.

Sam shaded her eyes and stared in the same direction Jen had turned.

Dad had ridden out early this morning in search of stray cattle. But the horse coming this way was too stocky to be Jeepers-Creepers, the Appaloosa he'd ridden. The rider's silhouette wasn't Dad's, either.

Ace's ears pricked to catch the sound of hooves. His long neigh vibrated through his barrel.

"Oh no," Sam muttered with a sigh.

Of all the people she'd rather not see, this rider topped the list.

Jen had obviously recognized him, too.

"What *is* it with him?" Jen called to Sam. "We're

surrounded by hundreds of acres of open range and he has to show up exactly where we are."

"He likes to humiliate me," Sam explained.

"Maybe he won't see you," Jen suggested, but she didn't sound hopeful.

Maybe.

If they were surrounded by a cloak of invisibility.

If they hadn't left a single hoof print on the desert floor.

If Ace grew little gold wings and flitted high into the sky.

Sam leaned forward against Ace's neck.

"This is all your fault, you know."

The bay gelding shook his mane and nickered as the dark rider loped closer.

With his black horse, black Stetson, and relentless approach, he looked like a bad guy in an old Western movie. And he was definitely coming their way.

Chapter Two ❧

$\mathcal{J}$ake Ely was no evil horseman. The youngest of six sons, he lived on Three Ponies Ranch, which bordered the Forsters' River Bend Ranch, and he'd been Sam's friend since childhood. Jake understood her love for horses better than anyone except Jen, and he'd stood beside her when she needed help.

But the price of Jake's help was merciless teasing, and her predicament, right this minute, couldn't have been more perfect for the mockery cowboys called "joshing."

She still had a minute until Jake reached the pond.

"Ace, be a buddy," Sam begged the horse. She settled into the saddle, let her boots drop to a normal position, then firmed her legs against him.

Silly nickered nervously when she saw Jake's Quarter Horse. Witch considered herself a queen among mares and she didn't mind proving the point with kicks and nips. But she got along fine with Ace.

"Let's go see Witch," Sam said, encouraging her gelding.

But it was already too late. Jake had drawn rein just a few feet away from Jen.

"Hey Jake," Jen said.

"Jen," Jake said, and he actually sounded friendly.

What's this? Sam wondered. Usually, Jake and Jen were rivals, sparring with words while Sam tried to keep them from actual arguing.

Jen had a great, sarcastic sense of humor, but she couldn't actually be enjoying the fix her best friend was in, could she?

"Ace won't come out of the water," Jen told Jake, and her voice carried to Sam much too clearly.

"Jen." Sam tried not to sound as if she were pleading. Couldn't Jen have made something up? Like, Sam was giving Ace a mud bath? As therapy for sore legs, or something?

"That a fact?" Jake asked.

"Keep riding, cowboy," Sam shouted at him. "I don't need your help."

Instead of jogging away, Jake leaned his forearm against his saddle horn. Beyond the cuff of his faded blue shirt his fingers tapped one at a time, as if pressing piano keys. Was that a sign of impatience or was Jake just thinking? The rest of him was still as he sighted past Witch's neck, studying Sam's situation.

"It'd be no trouble at all," Jake offered.

"We've got it handled," Jen said, but since she was a terrible liar, Jen's voice tilted up, like a question, and she gave a grimacing shrug in Sam's direction.

Then, both Jen's and Jake's voices dropped to inaudible levels.

Unfair! They were muttering, plotting her rescue without consulting her!

"Excuse me?" Sam shouted, but they didn't stop scheming.

Jake often called her "Brat." Sam bit her lower lip, thinking he should take it back for all the self-control she was showing now. A brat would have bragged that she could ride out of this silly mudhole whenever she felt like it, even if the logical part of her brain knew otherwise.

Jake rolled one shoulder, flexed his fingers, then unsnapped the leather loop that held his rope.

He was going to try to lasso Ace.

Sam's heart did a nosedive. Jake never missed. He'd rope Ace, then lead him from the water. She'd just sit still, along for the ride, like a child on a pony.

"Don't bother," Sam called to him.

"It's no bother," Jake replied. "Settin' a loop on him should be easy as lickin' butter off a knife."

Sam gritted her teeth.

Jake's dad was Shoshone, a native Nevadan. Jake's mother had been born in California. Jake had never lived anywhere he could have picked up that drawl. He only did it to make her crazy.

But she would *not* give him the satisfaction of scolding him. Instead, Sam closed her eyes as the loop sung in her direction. She only flinched when, at the last minute, Ace ducked his head.

"Why, you—!" Jen's gasp of disbelief could have been aimed at Jake or Ace.

All Sam knew was that the rope tightened around her arms, pinning her elbows against her ribs. Her legs clamped closed. Her wrists cocked up and her fingers scrabbled for the reins as Ace shied sideways and the taut rope pulled her from the saddle.

"No, no, noooo!"

Sam pitched face-first into the lake. Water gushed up her nose.

Boots down! she told herself. *Now, push up. Up.* A deluge of lake water rushed off her shoulders. Her boot soles slipped on the slimy footing, but she managed to stand.

The length of rope leading back to Jake flipped. The loop loosened. Sam bent forward, clawed her fingers through the circle of rope, and widened it.

She pushed it up over her head in time to glimpse Witch trying to bolt from the watery commotion.

"You *better* run!" Sam sputtered.

When she shook her head to clear her nose and ears, locks of wet hair splatted against her cheeks.

Unsteady on her boot soles, Sam staggered as she shouted, "You did that on purpose!"

Jake was an excellent roper. If he'd meant to lasso Ace, he would have done it.

"He dropped his head!" Jake shouted in denial.

Sam slogged through the water. She was almost ashore and Jake must have seen the fury in her eyes because he added, "No horse shies like that. How'd I know he was going to?"

Sam could hear her own loud breathing as she reached Jake and Witch. He must have been banking on her reluctance to hurt his horse, because he didn't ride away.

Jake was an expert roper. He never missed, but no one was perfect, right? Sam studied him for a clue that he'd done it on purpose.

"It was an accident," Jake insisted, but laughter rolled beneath the surface of his voice.

That's it, she thought. He wouldn't be laughing if he'd accidentally missed. Even though he managed to keep a straight face, she didn't believe him.

"Anyone can miss," he added.

Not this time, Sam thought. She made a fist and socked him in the leg.

"Now, Samantha, act like a lady," he scolded and actually brushed at the mud she'd smeared on his jeans.

Jen must have known that would send Sam over the edge.

"Oh, I'm out of here," Jen said, backing Silly away.

"Can't say that I blame you." Jake backed Witch, too.

Both mares, the black and the gold, stayed just out of Sam's reach.

"Come back here," Sam started, but then she thought of the laughable picture she must be making.

Hair dripping down her neck and into her eyes, walking stiff-legged because of her soggy jeans, she probably looked like a horror movie monster.

"I don't know what's gotten into you," Jake teased. "All I did for you was a favor."

Sam told herself to get a grip, because Jake was enjoying this way too much. She had to pretend it wasn't bothering her.

Sam closed her eyes, clenched her fists, and swallowed. She took one deep breath. Then another.

A sharp whistle sounded.

"Ace," Jake shouted, summoning the horse.

Don't move, Ace. Don't you dare take a single, solitary step. Sam said it silently, inside her head. If she'd said it aloud, would Ace have obeyed?

Sloshing legs and plopping hooves moved through the water behind her.

No. Ace was not just walking out of the lake because Jake had called him.

But he was.

"Good pony," Jake said.

"Go away," Sam said.

"Not talkin' to Ace, are you?"

"I'm talking to you!"

She would have yelled, except that Ace gave her such an energetic nudge between the shoulder blades, her words turned into a gasp and she barely kept from tripping.

"Guess I'll be riding along," Jake said.

"Where are you going, anyway?" Jen asked. "Gold Dust?"

Sam couldn't believe Jen sounded so conversational.

"Yep," Jake said.

"That's nice," Jen replied. Sam sent Jen brain waves not to ask why. Jake didn't like Linc Slocum, owner of the Gold Dust Ranch. If anything, he liked Linc's kids, Rachel and Ryan, even less.

"Matter of fact—" Jake began.

"We didn't ask!" Sam interrupted.

"I'm about to go trackin' some trackers."

What?

Jake meant to intrigue them, to tempt Sam or Jen into asking what he meant by that, of course.

Which trackers was he tracking? Sam wanted to know, but right now, with rivulets of mud tickling down her legs, all because of Jake, she wouldn't ask.

She flashed Jen a pleading look. They'd had their

ups and downs, but Jen proved herself a best friend by closing her lips in a purposely tight line, and rolling her eyes in pretend boredom.

Jen might be dying to know what Jake was talking about, especially since her father was foreman at the Gold Dust Ranch, but Jen backed Sam up.

Thank you, Sam mouthed. Jen gave a no-big-deal shrug.

Unfortunately, Jake didn't look a bit annoyed. He touched his hat brim in a polite good-bye. As he swung Witch away, Sam noticed Jake's glossy black hair, bound back with a leather tie.

It swayed against his shirt collar as Witch rocked from a walk into a lope.

Ace nickered after them, then looked at Sam with wide, surprised eyes as she snagged his reins.

"Don't play dumb with me," Sam told him. "You know why I'm mad at you."

Ace slung his head over her shoulder and rubbed his chin against her back. Sam sighed in frustration. If that wasn't a horse hug, she didn't know what was, and she couldn't resist his affection.

"He's saying it was all Jake's fault," Jen said.

"All except for that part where I was stranded in the middle of the lake in the first place." Sam rubbed Ace's neck. Water dripped from her sleeve.

"If you don't want to go for a ride water-logged, I don't blame you," Jen said. "I have to be home soon, anyway. My parents saved most of my chores for me.

Can you believe that? I'm off taking a college chemistry class during summer vacation and they couldn't brush a few ponies for me."

Jen made a face. "And they say that if I want to help out with HARP next week—which I absolutely do—I have to finish my work first."

"It will be so cool working with you on the HARP program," Sam said.

HARP was the Horse and Rider Protection program, which matched at-risk girls with captive mustangs that had been relinquished by their adoptive families. River Bend Ranch, with Sam's stepmother Brynna in charge, had been chosen to host the program for several weeks this summer.

Last week had been their first official session, and though only two girls had stayed in the new bunkhouse and Sam and Brynna had worked together as teachers, the week had been way more exciting than Sam had bargained for.

In fact, Sam had learned to watch where she stepped around the ranch. One of the HARP girls had been bitten by a snake, and though it hadn't been a rattler, Sam knew there were poisonous snakes around.

"Next week shouldn't be as crazy as last week," Sam told Jen. "I mean, Brynna will be back at work during the day, but I sort of know what to expect now." Sam felt a little guilty as she lowered her voice. "It's not just doing a good deed and playing with horses."

"I never thought it would be," Jen said. She blinked owlishly behind her glasses.

"Well, I did," Sam confessed. "Anyway, I'm pretty sure the three of us can handle it."

"Tell me how Brynna convinced Jake to do it, after he said he wasn't cut out to be a teacher."

"He needs the money," Sam said simply. "He and Darrell were able to make his mom's Honda look good as new after he crashed it trying to miss Jinx—"

"Hey," Jen interrupted when Sam mentioned the hard-luck horse Sam had ridden in a claiming race just days ago. "When do I get to see Jinx?"

"Maybe we can get someone to drive us to Sheriff Ballard's house," Sam said.

"That would be kind of weird," Jen said.

Sam gave a disagreeing hum, but she knew what Jen meant. Even though Sheriff Ballard was friendly before he'd purchased Jinx from the claiming race, you didn't just drop in on the local sheriff.

"For sure you'll see him at the Fourth of July parade," Sam said.

"And Jinx has what to do with Jake teaching for HARP?" Jen asked.

"Money," Sam reminded her. "Even though it wasn't his fault, Jake's car insurance has gone up big time."

Ace moved to the end of his reins and Sam clucked at him to keep his attention. She really should remount, but she was pretty sure she'd be even less comfortable in the saddle.

"That's not even fair," Jen said.

"No, but his parents say the extra dollars aren't in the family budget, so if he wants to drive—"

"—he has to pay for it," Jen finished. "Just like I have to go out and look for stray cattle because Linc Slocum was too lazy to hire cowboys for the roundup."

Sam nodded. The range was divided into sections. Each spring and fall, ranchers were responsible for bringing together the cattle—their own, and cows that had wandered from other ranches—on their sections.

Linc Slocum had neglected his part of the job this spring. Ever since the roundup had ended, calves from Gold Dust, River Bend, and Three Ponies ranches had been showing up unbranded.

"So, you'll be the responsible one, and Slocum gets off again," Sam said.

Jen nodded, then her face lit with an idea.

"You know what would be unbelievably cool? Oh wow," Jen paused. Sam could see that Jen, in her typically analytical way, was processing her idea before blurting it out. "It could work. You know our campout? What if we gathered strays at the same time—oh, and it could be a Father's Day present. So my dad and yours can quit worrying about all those unbranded calves."

Despite the warm June sun, goose bumps rose beneath Sam's wet clothes as a breeze passed by, but she nodded eagerly.

"We'll talk," Jen promised. "But you're starting to shiver. Time for you to get home," Jen said.

"It is," Sam said, not protesting her friend's maternal urging.

Slowly, movements made stiff by her sopping jeans, Sam lifted her boot to the stirrup and swung back into the saddle.

She was about to tell Jen good-bye when she heard a high, undulating wail.

Silly tossed her palomino head. Her brown eyes looked frightened behind a veil of flaxen mane.

"What was that?" Sam asked Jen.

"Not a coyote," Jen muttered. She turned Silly in a circle, distracting her from the sound.

Sam swallowed hard. The keening cry was like the one she'd heard before, but this time it not only sounded weirder—it was closer, too.

Chapter Three ❧

"It's just wind in the canyon. Now that the trees have leafed out, the acoustics are different." Jen's voice deepened as she stressed a logical explanation.

"You're probably right," Sam said, though Ace's ears pricked forward with interest. With a wave, she aimed Ace toward home.

The sun shone from directly overhead. Ace seemed to jog within his own shadow. If he'd sensed that howl from the hills was worth fearing, he'd forgotten about it.

Sam was nearly home when she saw Dad. From his lazy wave, it was clear he'd spotted her first.

She'd come to expect that.

A lifelong cowboy, Dad could scan the brown and

green vastness of the range and tell faraway rocks and bushes from cattle, deer, or mustangs. It sounded easy, but it wasn't. Sam couldn't count the number of times her heart had leaped up from spotting a wild horse, only to have it turn into a stunted pinion pine, dancing in the wind, when she got closer.

Dad swayed easily in the saddle as Jeepers-Creepers, his flea-bitten Appaloosa cow horse, descended a trail from the foothills.

Jeep seemed nervous. The rangy gray-and-white horse switched his rattail and looked behind him as if he feared he was being followed.

He was.

Baying and rushing, a pack of dogs skittered down the trail behind Jeep.

Dad didn't look back. He sent the Appaloosa surging forward, jumping ahead to level footing. Then, Dad turned Jeep to face the dogs.

And they *were* dogs, not coyotes or wolves. Black, white, speckled, and tan, the dogs moved in a blur. Sam couldn't tell how many there were. Four? Maybe five?

They circled silently now, except for loud sniffing. Could the hounds be planning their next move?

Sam pulled Ace to a stop. His forefeet danced. Did he want to bolt forward or retreat? Sam sat hard in the saddle, reins snug.

"Dad's got enough to worry about," she whispered to Ace.

Dad had Jeep under control, but the Appaloosa was scared. He tossed his head, straining the horse-hair reins in a straight line to his hackamore. His pink-rimmed eyes rolled white and his hooves' staccato tapping said Jeep was barely setting each hoof down before jerking it up again.

Dogs were predators.

Horses were prey.

Jeep knew that speed was his only defense. He wanted to flee, but as long as the dogs weren't snarling or biting, he'd trust Dad's orders. He wasn't allowed to bolt.

Sam knew why. If Jeep ran, the dogs would be on him.

"Get outta here!" Dad shouted at the dogs. "Go on, get!"

One dog fell back, hearing the authority in Dad's voice, but another dashed ahead, brushing Jeep's forelegs.

Jeep started to rear as the largest of the hounds jumped up. Dad slammed his weight against the horse's neck, trying to keep him down, so he'd have the balance of all four hooves.

With a low whinny, Jeep obeyed. Suddenly Dad gripped and lifted his coiled rope. In a backhand smack, he struck at the big dog, but not before it nipped the Appaloosa's nose.

It was too much.

Jeep was stronger than Dad was heavy. He

soared into a full rear, nose dripping blood. When the speckled hound leaped a second time, as if going for the horse's throat, Jeep tried to stand even taller. Then, he fell.

Dad! Sam thought. Fear tightened her throat. She couldn't yell, but she gave a kick and Ace galloped straight toward Jeep.

Sam had never seen Dad be thrown from a horse.

Hands tangled in Ace's mane, she leaned low, holding tight in case the dogs turned on her.

She'd fallen before. She'd seen Jake thrown, too. But not Dad. Ever.

A yelp split the rustling sounds of paws and claws. The pack was running away.

By the time Sam pulled Ace to a stop, dust hung in the hounds' wake. They'd retreated up the hill, back the way they'd come.

"Don't get down!" Dad warned her.

His voice lashed so loudly, Ace shied and sniffed, sucking in a wind scented with dogs and Jeep's blood.

When Jeep lurched to his feet, Dad held his reins, keeping the horse between himself and the hillside.

The Appaloosa blew through his lips, calmer now that another horse was near.

"You did pretty good," Dad said, giving Jeep's neck a hearty pat. Using his shirtsleeve, Dad swiped at Jeep's nose. "That cut's no big deal," he told the horse. "You'll forget about it before long."

Standing beside Jeep, Dad gripped both reins in his right hand while he slid his left over the horse's shoulder. He closed his eyes and grimaced, squatting instead of bending from the waist, to run his hand across Jeep's chest.

Dad's eyes darted from the hillside to Sam to his search for more wounds on the Appaloosa.

"Pretty excitin' there for a minute, wasn't it?" Dad asked Sam. His smile was white against his sun-browned skin, but Dad's eyes weren't happy. They weren't even relieved.

Sam's breath gusted out.

"Pretty terrifying," she corrected him. "Are you all right, Dad?"

"I'm kicking myself for being a fool. I never should have taken the scabbard off my saddle."

Sam shivered, and this time it wasn't from her damp clothes. When cougars had roamed the foothills last fall, Dad had put a rifle scabbard on his saddle. That was the only time she'd known him to ride out armed.

Did that mean he would have shot the dogs? Would he call Sheriff Ballard and have him capture them? Or would Dad think it was a one-time accident?

She didn't recognize the dogs, but maybe he would. Before she could ask, Dad took in her soaked clothing.

"What happened to you?" Dad asked.

"Ace decided to go for a swim," Sam said absently.

Dad wasn't moving right. He gave a short, humorless laugh. He pressed his lips together in a hard line as he lifted his boot toward Jeep's stirrup.

"Did Jeep fall on you?" Sam asked.

"Didn't you hear the yelp? He fell on that black-and-tan hound. Don't know how bad he hurt him, but that's what sent 'em runnin'."

Vaguely, Sam remembered the cry of a frightened dog. Next, she realized Dad hadn't really answered her.

"Maybe you should stay here and let me go get Gram, so you could ride back in the car," she suggested.

"Maybe I should, but then Jeep would think something had gone wrong," Dad said. "It could turn him spooky around dogs, and then what? If there's one thing we don't need around here . . ." Dad's voice trailed off, then he looked up and gave Sam a wink. "If I ride him in as usual, he might forget all about it. When I doctor his nose, he'll wonder what the fuss is about."

"Okay," Sam said dubiously.

Dad's boot was in the stirrup and he was about to swing his leg over for the other stirrup when Jeep shied off a step.

"Knock that off," Dad ordered.

His sternness turned the Appaloosa statue still,

but Sam saw a pale ring around Dad's mouth.

She'd been right. Dad was in pain.

"Dad, are you sure?" she asked as he gathered his reins.

"Let's go," he said, and Sam rode after him.

Chapter Four Ꮬ

The La Charla River glinted sapphire blue and its rills shone in the summer sun.

Sam's clothes had dried to a comfortable temperature and the countryside lay peaceful around them. Only the far-off bawling of a calf broke the silence and Dad rode with his usual ease.

It was hard to believe anything was wrong, but swelling marked the spot where the dog's fangs had slashed Jeep's tender nose.

"What are you going to do about those dogs?" Sam asked.

"I'm thinking," Dad said. "Goin' after a full-grown horse like that shows they've got some nerve. Wouldn't take much at all for them to bring down a calf or foal."

The image of Dark Sunshine's foal, just weeks old, flashed into Sam's mind.

"Tempest—" she began.

"—is safe," Dad assured her. "That corral fence goes down to the ground. You checked it yourself. And can you imagine the ruckus Blaze would set up if another dog trespassed on his territory?"

Dad was right. Blaze was the ranch dog. A Border Collie, he was devoted and fiercely protective when it came to River Bend Ranch.

"Do you think those dogs would go after the mustangs?" Sam asked.

"They might," Dad said.

"I think—I'm not sure—but I think I saw Moon nearby with a couple of mares," Sam said. In all the excitement, she'd almost forgotten.

"He's young," Dad said, "but the wild ones are probably safe. They're set up for attacks."

Sam's sensible side knew Dad was right. She'd seen the Phantom strike out with flashing teeth and lashing hooves.

But it was the time of year that wild stallions fought to add to their herds. Could a stallion watch for challengers every minute and still protect his mares and foals?

Sam loved dogs, but she wanted that pack off the range. Whoever had turned them loose was irresponsible and not very smart.

Dad's sigh snatched Sam's attention back. Even if he wouldn't admit it, Dad hurt from that fall. She knew that from experience.

"I'll put Jeep away for you, Dad," Sam said as the horses clopped across the wooden bridge to the ranch.

"Naw," Dad said, "I'll take care of both horses. Looks like you'll be cleaning that saddle till lunchtime, at least."

Sam gave Dad a sidelong glance. His expression was hidden by the shade from his Stetson, but it would have been hard to read anyway. Dad didn't like admitting he needed help.

Still, he *was* tougher than she was. Maybe she was exaggerating how shaken up he was by the fall.

"Okay," she agreed.

As they rode into the ranch yard, Blaze frisked around the horses' legs as usual.

Sam watched the horses for residual fear.

Ace only snorted, and though Jeep's back hooves clattered out of rhythm for a second, neither horse acted scared.

"That's a relief," Sam said, and Dad nodded.

Clearly, the horses didn't connect Blaze with that growling, snapping pack.

Sam dismounted and stripped off Ace's saddle. Balancing the saddle against one hip, she placed a hand on the warm, damp hair of Ace's back.

"Good boy," she whispered to the little mustang.

Red-brown hairs stuck to her hand as she stroked him, but she didn't care. "You could've gone nuts when those dogs showed up, but you took care of me."

Ace's head swung around and his lively eyes peered at her past his forelock. She made a kissing sound and he answered with a nod.

As she set off to work, Sam felt a rush of affection for Ace and her ranch life. So what if she didn't want to clean her saddle? It was better than cleaning her room.

The worst part of the chore was the way her damp jeans rasped her legs as she arranged herself and the saddle on the front porch, but she didn't want to go inside and tell Gram what had happened. She'd leave that up to Dad.

Blaze sniffed at her boots. Loudly.

"Don't ask why I smell like pond scum," she told him.

He didn't, but his nose continued to investigate as she washed mud from the leather with soap and water, then scrubbed it with a semidry sponge and more soap.

Blaze lost interest and trotted off to find Dad while Sam's stomach rumbled at the scent of Gram's cooking. It felt like a long time since breakfast.

Eager to finish before Gram called them in to eat, Sam wiped all the leather with neat's-foot oil and rubbed until the leather was glowing and supple once more.

She glanced up and saw Dad over by the barn.

What was he doing with that pitchfork? Looking kind of off balance, he pressed one hand to the small of his back as he extended the tool.

He'd dropped a saddle blanket, Sam realized, and he was pulling it closer with the fork.

He must be stiff already. Or maybe it hurt to bend over, as he usually would, to pick it up. Dad needed to take the afternoon off or at least swallow a few aspirin.

Dad wouldn't admit his discomfort to her, but Gram was his mother. She didn't miss much. She hoped Gram would talk some sense into him.

It wasn't long before Gram called them in for lunch.

"That's what smelled so good," Sam moaned as she saw Gram's brown-sugar baked beans. She wanted to spoon some into her mouth now, not waste time going upstairs to change.

Gram smiled as she glanced at Sam. When Gram turned back to the ham sandwiches on the cutting board, Sam felt relieved. Gram hadn't even noticed her bedraggled clothes.

"They do smell good, don't they?" Gram used the back of her wrist to push away a lock of gray hair that had escaped her tightly pinned bun. "It's a shame you won't be having any until you go change."

So she *had* noticed.

"I'm not that dirty," Sam protested as she spotted a big blue bowl of potato salad.

"Not for someone who's been rolling in the mud," Gram said. "But too dirty to sit at the table."

"Okay," Sam said, giving in.

Just before she turned to go, Sam noticed that though Gram had been talking to her, she'd also been eyeing Dad as he washed up for lunch.

"Your back's aching," Gram said, not giving Dad a chance to deny it. "What happened?"

Sam stopped with one hand on the swinging door to the living room.

"Couple dogs ran down from one of the trails and spooked Jeep."

Sam couldn't believe how Dad minimized what had happened. A couple of dogs? Spooked?

She crossed her arms and sent Dad a look. She'd be in big trouble if she did what he was doing.

"You go on upstairs and get into clean clothes," Dad said, but Gram hadn't missed their exchange.

"Out with it, Wyatt."

Sam kept moving, but just before the door swung closed she heard Gram say, "Tell me what happened, and I'm not taking 'no' for an answer."

Sam smothered a giggle and bolted up the stairs. It was so cool when Gram treated Dad like a kid, she didn't want to miss any more of his scolding than she had to.

By the time she'd changed and hurried back to the kitchen, Gram was sitting at the table. She wasn't sitting in her own chair, and the fingers of one hand touched her brow.

"My Lord, Wyatt," she murmured.

"It could have been bad," Dad agreed, then he and Gram stared at each other.

To Sam, it seemed as if they were picturing many outcomes for the attack, all of them violent.

Shaking her head, Gram stood, then began putting lunch on the table. As soon as she'd finished and Sam and Dad sat, Gram shook her head again.

"I'm calling Trudy," she said.

Trudy Allen had a wild horse sanctuary not far away and she was one of Gram's best friends.

"I'm thinking of that blind filly," Gram went on as she dialed.

"Faith," Sam gasped. Suddenly Sam knew Gram had pictured the dogs attacking the blind filly or Penny, her stepmother's blind mare. And what about small children? She couldn't think of any little kids in the area, but she'd bet there were some.

"Those yappy little dogs are no protection," Gram muttered, referring to Mrs. Allen's pets.

"There's Roman," Sam suggested, thinking of the liver-chestnut gelding who counted himself boss of the "unadoptable" mustangs roaming Mrs. Allen's pastures.

Dad was resolutely eating lunch, acting untouched by all of Gram's fuss.

"Dad?" Sam said.

"I'll take care of it," he said. "You can count on it."

Chapter Five ❧

"ℋorse on the porch."

Sam and Dad stared at Gram. Had she been talking to Mrs. Allen?

No. With the telephone receiver clamped between her ear and shoulder, Gram pointed toward the kitchen door.

As she did, hooves clopped on wood.

Then Sam heard hooves on dirt. Many hooves.

Once before, on the night of the fire, River Bend's horses had been freed from the ten-acre pasture. The horses had been gone all night, but in the morning, one had shown up on the ranch house's wide wooden porch. Ace.

He must be the horse on the porch now.

Grimacing, Dad pushed up from his chair at the table, but Sam darted past him.

"Go ahead," Dad said, "but take it slow."

Sucking in a breath, Sam took smaller, quieter steps, instead of bursting out the door as she'd been about to do.

It didn't help. The horses still spooked.

A sudden stomping—like the pounding at a pep rally in the school gym, when everyone stomped their feet—erupted on the porch. Ace couldn't be making all that noise by himself.

Sweetheart, Gram's aged pinto, had been right behind Ace, but now both horses backed off the porch, just missing the roof support posts.

Ace retreated so fast, he rammed into Sweetheart and she scolded him with a bite. The gelding cried out in surprise, then whirled toward the ranch entrance and bolted into a run. Sweetheart followed, limping on a foreleg for an instant before she loosened up and galloped after him and the other horses.

"They're all out," Sam called back to Dad.

Dad was at her elbow by now. Together they stared after the fleeing saddle horses. Ace and Sweetheart sprinted toward Popcorn, Jeep, and Strawberry.

Five horses were headed for open country.

Sam knew what she was doing with the rest of her day.

"Help me catch Amigo and Penny," Dad said.

She hadn't noticed the two sorrels milling next to the barn corral, uttering distressed nickers to Dark Sunshine and Tempest.

"Tell you what," Dad said. "Saddle up Amigo and trail them. With any luck, Ross and Pepper will run across 'em and push 'em on home, but if they don't, you can take a try at it."

Goose bumps pricked her arms and legs like a thousand cold, tiny needles. Dad was sending her out alone to bring back the saddle horses. Did he really expect her to be able to do it?

She tried to look confident, but Dad must have seen her hesitation.

"Only one way you learn to be a buckaroo," Dad told her, "and that's the hard way."

Sam almost stopped breathing.

A buckaroo wasn't just a cowboy. A buckaroo never drove when he could ride, never lost pride in his skills, and never let his ranch become a farm.

Sam only knew three buckaroos and they were all men: Dad, Jed Kenworthy, and Jake.

Being a buckaroo wasn't a matter of bloodlines, either. Jake's dad, Luke, was a good rider and rancher, but he also worked for a mining company in town. Luke wasn't a buckaroo, but Jake definitely was.

Once, Sam had heard Dad tell Brynna that he knew Jake for a buckaroo the first day he saw him mount an unbroken horse.

"He was so good, so soon, it was amazing," Dad

had said. And that's why he'd hired Jake to help with horses.

Sam wondered if she'd misunderstood Dad when he said *she* could be a buckaroo.

There was no time to ask.

She grabbed the halter and lead rope hanging over the hitching rail and strode toward Amigo. The old gelding tossed his graying muzzle skyward and rolled his eyes, but he didn't resist.

Penny, Brynna's copper-bright mare, was another story. Confused by the chaos, she squealed and rose into a half rear when Dad stood before her.

"Hey, little girl, you get back now. You're going nowhere. Brynna'll have my hide if I lose you."

The blind mare's ears pricked forward. Was it Brynna's name that made her stop rearing and shift from hoof to hoof?

While the mare calmed down, Dad kept talking to Sam.

"I'll be along on Penny, soon as I check the lock on that gate," Dad said as he slipped a rope around the mare's neck and led her into the barn stall.

Sam grabbed the tack that was still sitting out on the porch. With luck, it would fit, so she wouldn't have to go to the barn in search of Amigo's gear.

Close enough, Sam thought as she adjusted the headstall to Amigo's larger head. She smoothed on the saddle blanket, hefted the saddle, and grunted as she boosted the saddle onto Amigo's back. The cinch had to be fastened on a looser notch, but the saddle fit fine.

Sam managed to mount, in spite of feeling as if a giant hand held her by the ribs and waggled her back and forth. Was it her heartbeat? Her runaway pulse? Or the realization that Dad thought she could be a buckaroo?

He hadn't made any big deal over it. In fact, he acted as if he hadn't said it at all, but Dad touched his hat brim and lifted his chin toward the range.

See you out there, his gesture indicated, but as she rode away, Sam heard Dad mutter, "I know I closed that danged bolt."

Amigo was taller than Ace, and narrower. Although Sam knew the gelding was well fed, age had whittled him down. He was about fifteen years old and, according to Dallas, the best cow horse in the state.

There. Just as they jogged off the bridge, Sam saw the brown-and-white blur that was Sweetheart. Gram's mare trailed the dust raised by the other horses, and Amigo was eager to catch up.

It looked as if the saddle horses were slowing, spreading out, meandering with indecision. Would they follow the river toward the Three Ponies Ranch or cross the highway and head for Deerpath Ranch?

"Whoa, boy," Sam told Amigo. "Let's wait a minute and see what they do."

If the horses made a break for the road to Deerpath

Ranch and the Blind Faith Mustang Sanctuary, they'd be easier to catch. Mrs. Allen's road was fenced on both sides. Sam knew, because she'd helped build that fence.

But a sprint for Deerpath Ranch meant the horses would cross the highway. Though there wasn't likely to be much traffic, five horses could get into a lot of trouble if there were.

No, even though it would be tougher to gather them, Sam hoped the horses would keep moving along the river toward Three Ponies Ranch.

Amigo tossed his head against the reins, eager to follow the other horses.

Sam smooched to Amigo. He swiveled one ear to listen, but she could feel his impatience.

"Let them get settled," she told him. "Then we'll just herd them back toward home."

Finally she let Amigo start toward the others. She kept him at a walk until, up ahead, Strawberry veered into the river.

They were near enough now that Sam heard the mare blow through her lips as she lowered her head to drink.

Sam sighed as first Jeep, then Ace and Sweetheart followed Strawberry. Finally Popcorn joined them, grazing on the soft summer grass hidden among the riverside stones.

"Easy, easy," Sam told Amigo.

By the time they reached them, the horses showed

no signs of bolting.

Tree-strained sunlight dappled their backs and they barely raised their heads at Amigo's approach.

Popcorn lowered himself into the shallows and rolled in the mud.

It wasn't the first time Sam had seen the albino gelding change his coat from milky brightness to a calico of green and brown streaks from mud and river grass. Popcorn lurched upright and shook like a dog, splattering them with drops of muddy water.

Still, Sam didn't rush the horses.

A taste of freedom could make them hungry for more or, if she gave them half an hour to graze and wade, they might be willing to mosey on home.

At last she reined Amigo behind the group and gradually rode closer. The horses moved off in the general direction of the ranch.

So far, so good. Sam scanned the empty range for distractions. No cattle, no cars on the highway.

Strawberry snorted at the flick of a ground squirrel disappearing behind a boulder, and Sam leaned forward in the saddle. For some reason, the saddle herd followed the roan mare as their leader. If she made a break for open country, they'd be right behind her.

The horses kept moving. If everything stayed this way, she could bring them home.

Ace was the first to break into a jog. His bay head swung as if he were checking the mountain range for mustangs, but he followed Strawberry.

Sam increased the pressure of her legs just slightly and Amigo lengthened his strides. All of the horses fell into a lazy jog toward home.

Hooves made sucking sounds in the mud, struck submerged rocks, then dry dirt. Ears up, knees lifting, Strawberry began loping toward the bridge over the La Charla River.

"Almost there, almost," Sam murmured as Popcorn, who'd stayed toward the back of the herd, broke into a lope and caught up with Strawberry. With a quick flattening of her ears, she told him to back off, and though he was definitely headed for River Bend Ranch, he shortened his strides and didn't pass the invisible barrier that ran even with the roan mare's tail.

They were almost there when the metallic glitter of a truck, approaching from the direction of Linc Slocum's Gold Dust Ranch, caught Sam's eye.

Ace stopped. Ears pricked so intently that the tips trembled, he stared at the champagne-colored truck, looked away after the other horses, then considered the truck again, as if he couldn't believe his eyes.

It figured. Linc Slocum was the richest rancher in this part of Nevada, maybe in the entire state, and though he longed to be considered a real cowboy, Sam was pretty sure it would never happen.

If there was a way to mess up the business of ranching—of dealing with the land, animals, and

people who considered the high desert their home —
Linc Slocum would stumble upon it. Many of his mis-
deeds were done on purpose, but just as many were
the worst sorts of accidents.

Like this. If Ace caused a commotion because he
perceived some threat from the vehicle, if he caused
the other horses to wheel and run for the mountains,
she'd have Slocum to blame. Or at least Slocum's
vehicle, she thought, because now, as it inched nearer,
she saw that Linc wasn't at the wheel. The driver's silhouette wasn't bulky and broad like Linc's. Could it
be Ryan? Maybe, although he'd stayed so close to
Hotspot and her foal, it would be a surprise.

The dark outline seemed more familiar as it drew
closer, but Sam looked away. If she played her cards
right, she could have the horses across the bridge and
headed for home pasture before the truck reached
them.

"It's up to you, boy," Sam told Amigo, and the
sorrel settled into a swinging lope, the gait he used
to herd cattle, which could stay placid as a rocking
chair or explode into a burst of speed certain to cut
across the path of any animal making a break away
from the herd.

She'd done it. The horses were trotting across the
bridge, hooves hammering an announcement that
she'd brought them safely home, when suddenly Sam
recognized the driver.

Jake. She straightened with such surprise that

Amigo snorted and his smooth stride switched to a slower, rougher gait.

"It's okay, Amigo," she told the old horse, touching his flaxen mane for assurance. "Everything's okay, except Jake's apparently gone *loco*."

Chapter Six ⌇

Something big and metal jangled as it was jarred around in the back of the truck. Sam heard a howl and shivered. Then the sounds came together, painting a picture in her mind.

Dogs in a cage. *Those* dogs.

All at once, she was relieved not to be riding Ace. The little horse had wanted to battle them as if they were predators.

Why were those dogs in Slocum's truck? And why was Jake driving it?

You'll never know if you don't ask, she told herself, but she couldn't rush the horses just to satisfy her curiosity.

The truck stopped about a hundred yards away.

Idling, the vehicle sounded like a small factory.

When all the horses had crossed the bridge and showed no signs of turning back, Sam reined Amigo toward the truck.

If you didn't know Jake, his set jaw would just look stubborn, but Sam could tell he wasn't gloating over driving Slocum's truck. He was embarrassed by the loud, flashy vehicle.

The dogs yapped and yodeled as Sam rode closer. Amigo made a cautious, inquiring snort, and Sam felt a bit scared.

"They can't get out, can they?" she called.

Jake rested his arm on the sill of the driver's window.

"'Course not," he said. Hatless, he pushed back a clump of black hair that had fallen over his brow. Sam noticed his faded blue shirtsleeve was rolled up. "Never knew you to be scared of dogs."

"Just *those* dogs," Sam said. Then, slapping one hand over her nose, she recoiled. "What's that smell?"

"Sardines," Jake said. "They're hunting dogs. I couldn't chase 'em down on foot. I tracked 'em so far, then set up their cage—"

Their cage? Did that mean the dogs were usually kept in it? Despite their ferocity, Sam felt a little sorry for them.

Jake's eyes slid sideways from hers, and she guessed he felt the same. "—and used a scent I was pretty sure would carry."

"It carries, all right," Sam said, still cupping her hand over her nose.

Sam stood in her stirrups to look into the back of the truck, through the narrow bars on the cage. Open-mouthed and excited, the dogs wagged their tails.

Even though they'd probably gulped down the sardines an hour ago, they were panting fish-scented breath.

Up close, they didn't look so scary. The black-and-tan hound's floppy ears and sad-looking eyes made him almost cute. But he'd been the one that had leaped snarling into Jeep's face and slashed his tender nose.

"Back by the lake, when you said you were track-ing trackers . . ." Sam paused as Jake began nodding. "They were the reason you went to Gold Dust Ranch? So, they're Linc Slocum's dogs?"

"Yep," Jake answered.

"You're lucky you weren't riding Witch," Sam said. She imagined Jake's Quarter Horse mare tram-pling the dogs.

"Not lucky." Jake's flat tone hinted he'd caught the dogs with skill and planning. "Also might've been a chore to bring 'em home on horseback."

Of course. Sam winced at Jake's logic. It was just that she was so used to picturing him as a rider.

"They attacked Jeep."

Jake interrupted his level stare with a blink, then smiled. "*Attack*'s a pretty strong word."

"Talk to Dad," Sam said.

"Wyatt saw it?"

"Dad was riding Jeep"—Jake's only sign of surprise was the way his hand lifted from the windowsill, then flattened again, but Sam knew he wanted to hear more—"not far from High Grass Canyon," she went on. "The whole pack came down from behind him. That black-and-brown one jumped up and bit Jeep on the nose. When Jeep went over backward, Dad went with him. He was thrown clear."

Jake gave a quiet whistle of amazement. "Never knew Wyatt to come off a horse 'less he meant to."

"I know," Sam said. "That's why I'm kinda scared of them."

She stared at the dogs again. All three tails wagged furiously at her attention.

Typical. Jake didn't ask if Dad was all right. He assumed she'd tell him if there was more he needed to know. Instead, he seemed to mull over the dogs' behavior.

"They're deerhounds," Jake said slowly. "A blue tick, a Walker, and some kind of pointer."

"I don't care what they are, or why he has them," Sam snapped.

"Calm down, Brat."

"I'm calm. And I don't blame the dogs, exactly, but you wouldn't be so understanding if you'd seen them, Jake."

"Like werewolves, were they?" Jake meant it as a

joke, but she could tell his heart wasn't in it. He was as shaken as she was by Dad's fall.

"No . . . like predators," Sam told him.

If Jake was right, the dogs had been trained to hunt. Maybe even bred to hunt. And, knowing Slocum, he wasn't using them the right way.

"Why does he have them?" Sam asked. "I bet they're part of some wild scheme like the buffalo."

Jake shrugged, but Sam could see that the memory of Slocum's herd of bison—which he'd purchased to lure hunters to a Wild West resort he was planning—didn't sit well.

Linc Slocum had known nothing about the bison. He'd tried to herd them like cattle and they'd escaped.

Just like these dogs, which might have passed for family pets.

Yawning, the black-and-white speckled hound collapsed to the floor of the cage and rolled onto its back. Tail wagging, it begged Sam to scratch its belly.

"I can see through your disguise," she muttered, then suddenly she remembered the hounds Linc had rented to pursue the cougars last fall.

They'd been speckled like this dog, and they'd helped Linc corner a mother cougar. He'd shot her, leaving her adolescent cub to fend for himself.

Sam swallowed hard. She'd been riding Strawberry in Arroyo Azul when the young cougar had pounced.

She remembered the pain between her shoulder

blades and the terror of being overwhelmed by a wild animal.

No thanks to Linc, she and Strawberry had survived the attack.

Why couldn't Linc see that his mistakes led to disaster way too often? Why didn't he care?

"Don't underestimate them," Sam told Jake. "Those dogs are dangerous."

Suddenly the lazing hound jumped to his feet. Then they all began barking. An answering bark came from River Bend Ranch. Blaze was fiercely protective, but he wouldn't stand a chance against three trained hunters.

"I'd better get going," she said, gathering her reins. "But I think you should tell Linc about Dad."

Jake opened his mouth to speak, then closed it. He wouldn't enjoy giving Linc bad news. In fact, he'd hate it. Jake rarely spoke two sentences in a row to anyone. But Sam knew Jake would tell Slocum, because it was the right thing to do.

As soon as she reached the bridge's midpoint, Sam's eyes began searching for Dad. He'd promised to follow her, but once her horse clopped into the ranch yard, Sam realized he was nowhere to be seen.

The saddle horses had wandered into their pasture on their own, so Sam dismounted and locked the gate behind them.

It was a mystery how they'd escaped. She examined

the lock and it worked the same as always.

Dad would never forget to lock the gate. Neither would she, or anyone else on the ranch.

It was a rule of ranch life that open gates stayed open, closed gates stayed closed. You learned the hard way—by wasting hours going after wandering animals—not to forget.

Sam led Amigo to the hitching rail, tossed his reins over it, then went looking for Dad.

It wasn't just because she wanted his words of praise, she told herself. She wondered how he was feeling after that fall.

Dad wasn't in the barn, though Penny was, alert and ready to return to the ten-acre pasture. So, Dad hadn't ridden after her.

He wasn't in the tack room, and though she knocked at the bunkhouse door and called for him, there was no answer there, either.

Dad must be in the house. She'd only made it halfway there, when Gram came out on the porch.

"You got all of them, I see." Gram's arm circled Sam's shoulders in a hug. "You've come a long way since this time last year."

Sam smiled so hard, she felt a twinge in her cheeks, but Gram didn't give her long to gloat.

"Now, I need you to weed around the base of these morning glories," Gram said, pointing to vines with tightly closed blue flowers that twined up around the rabbit-proof fence that protected Gram's garden.

"Okay," Sam said. "But where's Dad? I need to tell him—"

"And when you're through with that, weed inside the garden itself, but those are carrots," she said, pointing to feathery greens just showing above the dirt, "and those are radishes. Don't pull them up by mistake."

"Okay," Sam said, again, "but shouldn't I tell Dad—"

"Then," Gram continued, with forced patience, "you can bring them some water. Plants can't pull up roots and go looking for it themselves, you know."

"Are you just going to keep giving me chores till I stop asking about Dad?" Sam asked, exasperated.

"Now, honey, why would I do that?" Gram asked.

Sam didn't guess aloud, but she'd bet Dad was taking a forced rest. He might be an adult, but Gram was still his mother.

"I might as well tell you what I told your father," Gram admitted. "He's no good to any of us all crippled up."

Gram tried to sound harsh, but Sam wasn't fooled.

"You made him take a nap, didn't you?"

"I might have suggested a hot shower and some aspirin," Gram admitted. "And since he was upstairs anyway, I mentioned it would do him good to get off his feet."

"I'm amazed, Gram," Sam said. "Dad never rests."

"You're old enough to know that fall shook him

up a bit," Gram confided.

Bone-deep fear chilled Sam. It had been years since she'd really thought about something happening to Dad.

Sam remembered her own awful fall. She'd been unconscious and they'd feared brain damage. And Mom had died from her accident. . . .

"He's fine," Gram insisted, squeezing Sam's arm. "If you'd heard how many times I had to promise to wake him if he nodded off, you wouldn't worry a bit."

"Shall I go tell him I'm back?" Sam asked.

Gram shook her head. "I heard him cross the bedroom floor and look out the upstairs window just before you rode in."

Sam shivered, but in a good way. It made her proud to know Dad had watched as she brought River Bend's horses home.

Chapter Seven ❧

"Black as midnight with two fine mares running alongside." Linc Slocum muttered the words as he swung high-gloss Western boots free of his champagne-colored truck.

Sam was the only one who heard him. Instantly, she knew he was describing New Moon.

In Gram's garden, Sam stood and wiped soil-coated hands on her jeans. Who was Linc talking to? It was almost dusk. Gram was inside cooking. Brynna had only been home a few minutes when Dad had whisked her off to the barn. Sam knew they were talking about the dogs and Dad's accident.

Linc carried a green plant potted in a white plastic container. Sam guessed it was for Dad's sickroom.

Jake must have told Linc Slocum about the dogs' attack.

Forget the carrots and radishes, Sam thought. Before Dad and Brynna confronted Linc about his dogs, she wanted to hear about the Phantom's son.

"Anybody here?" Linc called out. Leaving his truck door open, he started across the ranch yard, ankles wobbling.

"I am," Sam said. As she hurried toward him she noticed he was wearing even stranger clothes than usual.

Linc Slocum usually dressed like a city slicker playing cowboy, but today his yellow shirt with its silver-stitched yoke was tucked into pants patterned with tan camouflage. He'd stuffed his pant cuffs into his boots and the material puffed beneath his knees. Did he think he was dressed for hunting?

"You saw a black mustang?" Sam asked, shooting a quick glance at the barn to verify they were still alone.

"Yep, never seen this one before. Bet he could give that white stud a run for his money."

Sam knew Slocum was trying to taunt her into defending the Phantom, but she refused to take the bait.

"Where'd you see the black horse?" Sam tried not to sound like she was too interested.

"Let me think." Slocum let his eyes focus on space

as he trapped the potted plant between his ribs and elbow, then used both hands to heft his belt.

Strong belt, Sam thought as Linc's bulging belly lifted with the tooled leather.

"Here," he said, straightening a few mashed leaves on the plant before handing it to her.

Sam took the plant, but she'd bet Gram would say this was a sorry excuse for an apology.

"Seems to me that crowbait was by that path up to Grass Gulch," Linc said, finally.

Crowbait. She hated the expression some people used for wild horses, but she was only distracted for a few seconds.

There was no Grass Gulch around here.

"Long Grass Valley?" she suggested.

"Yeah, that's it," Slocum agreed.

Sam hoped Linc wouldn't notice her trembling hands as they clutched the plant.

Dad had been riding out of Long Grass Valley when the dogs had rushed down behind him. Even though she knew Jake had trapped those dogs and she'd seen them caged with her own eyes, Sam worried about New Moon.

"Linc," Brynna said as she left the barn and strode across the ranch yard.

Brynna's no-nonsense voice sounded like an accusation instead of a greeting. Sam knew she'd hear no more about the black mustang. At least for a while.

Brynna's manner was icy. Sam could feel it from here.

If Linc had arrived ten minutes earlier, he might have had a chance to break the news of his dogs' mistake to her. But he was too late for that and too early for her anger to have worn off.

"Now, B.," Dad cautioned, using his nickname for Brynna. He would have had better luck talking to the barn wall.

In a khaki uniform with her red hair french braided down her back, Brynna strode toward them.

Anyone could see Brynna's anger was still building. For once, Linc seemed to recognize it.

"I got it coming," he said when she was still a few yards off. "I want to pay for any inconvenience I've caused."

Linc fumbled a checkbook out of his pocket.

Sam couldn't believe Slocum wasn't apologizing. Instead, he was trying to pay for Dad's pain.

"Uh, and Jed mentioned I might want to bring something, so . . ." he pointed to the plant Sam held.

If Sam weren't so mad, she'd feel sorry for an adult who was so clueless.

Dad and Brynna stood, speechless, and Linc gave a nervous laugh.

"Any kinda lecture you want to give me, have at it. Jake Ely says my dogs spooked Wyatt's horse and left him pickin' stickers out of his pants. Don't blame you for being peeved."

Then, Linc laughed.

"Sorry about that." He cleared his throat, but gloating flavored his apology. Usually it was Linc, not Dad, who found himself afoot on the range. It was clear Linc found the switch amusing.

Brynna wasn't laughing. Her freckles disappeared on her scarlet-flushed face. Her lips turned white from pressing together.

Finally, she spoke.

"Are you aware"—Brynna's voice vibrated with rage—"that it's against state law to hunt deer with dogs?"

"Yeah, now that you mention it, Jed clued me in, right after I went and bought 'em."

Slocum looked down at his boots, shaking his head, then peered up, as if he expected sympathy.

Fat chance, Sam thought.

"Not to mention," Brynna pressed on, "county statutes prohibit dogs from running at large—"

"Guess I figured you and your boys couldn't be everywhere at once, now, can ya?"

Brynna's eyes widened and her lips parted in disbelief.

What? Outrage screeched in Sam's mind. Had Slocum really just admitted he didn't mind breaking the law, as long as he wasn't caught and punished?

"With hundreds of miles of nothing out there . . ."

Slocum gave a short *heh, heh* sort of laugh, "don't figure the sheriff's got time to search me out to enforce that rule."

"It's not a rule," Brynna corrected him. "It's a law."

Slocum shrugged. "A darned silly law."

Sam forgot about asking Linc for more information on New Moon.

"You wouldn't think it was silly if you'd seen Dad's horse fall, like I did."

Silence sizzled around them as Linc searched for a comeback.

"Thing is," Dad said, at last, "they're gonna get shot."

Linc leaned back, thumbs hooked through his straining belt. "Is that a threat?"

"'Course not," Dad said. "But no one takes kindly to dogs bitin' his livestock."

Not to mention what might have happened if Dad had fallen and rolled. What if all the dogs had attacked him at once?

"But you'd actually shoot my dogs?" Linc persisted.

"I wouldn't like doin' it," Dad said. "But if they brought down one of my calves or if they were about to attack my horse or yours"—he nodded at Linc—"you bet I would."

Linc's jaw dropped in astonishment.

"What if they'd spotted a child instead of Wyatt

and Jeep?" Brynna's tone soared uncharacteristically. "Those dogs—" She stopped.

Dad's arm circled Brynna's shoulders, and she took a deep breath. When she continued, she sounded calmer.

"If your dogs attacked a person, you could be looking at jail time, Linc. If they should go feral—"

"They won't," Linc promised. "They're valuable dogs."

So what? Sam thought. What did price have to do with anything? If the dogs had escaped once, they could do it again.

"Their names are kind of common, but they're bred and trained in Louisiana," he bragged. "And they cost me a pretty penny, let me tell you. Gator, he's the bluetick, kind of a speckledy one?" Linc looked at Sam and she nodded. "Then there's Bub. He's the pointer, and Shirley is the boss of 'em both, she's the black-and-tan Walker hound."

"If they turned feral," Brynna continued coldly, "they would be exceedingly dangerous. They've been trained to hunt, you say, so that's what they'll do. Feral dogs don't have the natural fear of man that wolves and coyotes do."

Brynna was right. The dogs had scattered only when Jeep had fallen on a member of the pack.

"I'll alert the Elys, Trudy Allen, and Sheriff Ballard—" Brynna began.

"Aw, now, there's no sense doing that," Linc said.

"It would be negligent not to," Brynna insisted. "Trudy Allen has that blind foal—"

"I just don't think they'll bother the horses. I think this"—Linc motioned toward Dad—"was a one-shot deal. I mean, horses are just like big dogs, aren't they? I don't see any reason they can't get along."

Although Brynna's face flushed even darker at Slocum's statement, she didn't bother educating him. She just finished her sentence.

"—and her grandchildren come to visit, too."

Brynna crossed her arms in a rigid bar at her waist, waiting.

"I promise my dogs won't get out again." Linc's voice overflowed with mock patience. He raised his right hand as if swearing in court.

"Huntin' dogs want to hunt," Dad said.

"I've got a dog handler," Linc protested. "His name's Karl."

Sam looked over in time to see Brynna's eyebrows arch in surprise.

"He wasn't around today," Linc said, shrugging. "But Karl keeps them in line."

Sam had to call Jen. That's all there was to it. Jen lived on Gold Dust Ranch where her dad, Jed Kenworthy, was Slocum's foreman. They'd know the dogs and their handler, Karl. If he even existed.

Judging by Dad's and Brynna's expressions, they

hadn't heard of a newcomer, either.

"I'm going to take this inside, okay?" Sam said, holding up the plant.

"Yeah," Dad told her, then nodded at Linc and said, "Thanks."

Sam hurried toward the house. She'd caught Linc Slocum lying more than once. This time it should be easy.

Sam's nose tingled at the aroma of the sauce Gram was stirring.

"Oh, yum," Sam said as she placed the potted plant in the middle of the kitchen table.

"Burritos for dinner," Gram said. "I should be making better use of that cooking class I took in New Mexico. What do you think?" she asked as Sam stared into the dark-red chili sauce.

"I think I may start drooling if I don't call Jen right now."

As she dialed, Sam summed up Linc's conversation with Brynna and Dad for Gram.

Gram shook her head. "That man's more irresponsible than a teenager."

Sam felt her mouth curve in a lopsided smile, but just then Jen answered the phone.

"Have you dried out yet?" Jen teased.

"Oh yeah. You'll never guess what happened on my way home."

After she told Jen about Dad's accident, Sam asked Jen to tell her all she knew about the dogs and their handler.

Jen hesitated. "I can't say much," she mumbled. "Mom might think this falls into the 'don't bite the hand that feeds you' category."

There was such a thing as being too polite, wasn't there? Sam twisted the phone cord, impatiently.

"Hold on. She's on her way out to hang laundry," Jen hissed.

"I'm patient," Sam said between gritted teeth. "I can wait."

Gram was cutting beef into bite-sized pieces for burritos, but she didn't pretend not to be listening. She smiled when Sam claimed to be patient, then gave her two onions, a cutting board, and a knife.

"So you don't get bored waiting," Gram said softly, though she knew Sam hated to peel onions.

After a full minute of silence, peeling, and sniffing away tears the onions brought to her eyes, Sam heard Jen take a long breath.

"The guy's a sleaze," Jen announced.

"It figures," Sam said. "Why didn't you tell me about him before?"

"I only met him once, and if he's the dogs' handler, he's controlling them—or not—by remote control."

"What do you mean?"

"Right after Linc hired him, the guy left," Jen said.

Knife poised in midair, Sam thought that over.

"Mince them," Gram whispered.

Sam rolled her watering eyes, but she didn't protest. She was too busy wondering why Linc had lied.

"You know how everyone's always saying Linc needs more cowhands, but he doesn't hire any?" Jen asked.

"Except that creep Flick," Sam put in.

"Right, and—hey, are you crying?" Jen asked incredulously.

"Chopping onions," Sam said with a sniff.

"Oh, okay. So you know how Flick turned out to be a criminal? This guy Karl—I don't know his last name—is the same sort of lowlife."

Sam believed her. Though she was only fourteen, Jen had the mind of a scientist. Instead of jumping to conclusions, she analyzed situations. If Jen said Karl the Dog Man was a crook, Sam was 99 percent certain he was.

Sam's pulse seemed to buzz in her wrists.

Linc Slocum had hired Flick to capture the Phantom. Why had he hired Karl?

Sam told herself to stop worrying. Jen had said Karl was gone.

"If this guy comes back, is he a good enough cowboy that he and your dad can handle the Gold Dust herd alone?"

Jen didn't answer. Her words came out in a tumble.

"Mom's done with the laundry and I'm supposed to be dusting furniture. I can see her through the window and she's coming this way. Gotta go."

Then, just before she hung up, Jen added something Sam couldn't quite make out. As the receiver clicked down, Sam tried to replay the words.

But they didn't make much sense, because it sounded as if Jen had said, "Karl's no cowboy. No way in the whole wide world."

Chapter Eight ❧

*G*ram looked at Sam with open curiosity.

"So what did Jennifer have to say?" Gram asked as she placed the meat into a cast-iron pot to brown.

"She didn't know much about the dogs or Karl, the guy who's supposed to be their handler. Jen met him, but she said he didn't act like a cowboy and she never saw him work. He was there one day and gone the next."

Gram didn't comment. She just carried on with dinner.

"Put those"—Gram nodded at the onions Sam had cut—"in with the meat."

Sam used the dull edge of the knife to sweep the onions off the cutting board and into the pot. As the onions sputtered, Sam's mind remained on the dogs.

Linc had come close to admitting only Karl knew how to control the hunting hounds. And Jen said he'd vanished. That didn't make sense, and it made her worry.

Of course, Dad, Jed Kenworthy, and the Elys would try to protect the cattle and horses on the three ranches bordering the La Charla River. But what would happen to the mustangs? If those dogs were fearless enough to attack a horse with a rider, tackling a foal would be like play.

The Phantom, New Moon, Yellow Tail, and the other mustang stallions would watch for raids on their bands, but could the foals keep up with a fleeing herd?

Sam gnawed her lower lip. What could she do?

Only when the onions and meat sputtered and a spatter of hot shortening hit her hand did Sam step back.

She almost collided with Blaze. The dog frisked around Dad and Brynna as they came into the kitchen.

"Well, that was a useless apology," Brynna said.

Dad shrugged. "Might be the best he can do."

Brynna gave a groan of disbelief.

"Wyatt, he wasn't sorry! Linc Slocum wants what he always does—his own way. He doesn't care about other people, animals, the land, or anything else. And what," Brynna asked as she pointed an accusing finger at the plant in the middle of the table, "is this about?"

Sam laughed. Brynna was right. Buying a potted plant for Dad was kind of silly.

"I'll rescue the poor thing," Gram said. "There's a sunny spot in the living room that might suit it."

"The apology isn't the point," Brynna said loudly. Then, as if she'd run out of anger, she sank into her chair at the table. She leaned back and tilted her head to look up at Dad. "I wouldn't accept his apology anyway, not when *you* got thrown."

"Jake was shocked, too," Sam said.

Dad gave her a wry smile. "So you been announcin' I fell off my horse."

"Only to Jake," Sam rushed to tell him. "And only because he trapped those dogs and I thought he should know to be careful."

"I'm joking, honey. A man's pride don't count for much in a situation like this."

Was Dad still joking? Sam couldn't tell.

"Where are you hurt?" Brynna asked sternly.

"I've already been seen to by an expert," Dad said, looking toward Gram as she heated tortillas on a griddle.

Brynna followed Dad's glance. When she still didn't look satisfied, Sam explained what she'd seen.

"Jeep reared and went over backward," Sam said. As the attack played out in her mind all over again, she used her hand to show the Appaloosa falling like a huge tree. "Dad's shoulder hit first, then he and Jeep sort of pressed the black-and-tan dog—"

"That would be Shirley," Dad said.

Brynna ignored Dad's light tone.

"So Jeep fell on top of you?" Brynna asked.

"No, I kicked free of the stirrups before my leg got trapped under him. That's why I fell off." Dad looked thoughtful, as if he was weighing his decision. "If I'd stayed in the saddle, I might have ridden through it. That mighta been best, 'cause it sure scared me when he didn't get up."

"What?" Sam asked. "It seemed like he got up right away."

Dad shook his head. "You were busy with Ace. That little mustang wanted to go after those dogs and teach 'em some manners, didn't he?"

Brynna still didn't smile.

"One rein got pinned under Jeep, so he couldn't swing his head to get up," Dad explained. "Took him a minute to figure out what was going on, but he didn't panic. Lucky they were split reins. Soon as I fished that one out from under him, Jeep just lurched up on all fours."

Brynna's sigh coincided with the arrival of their dinner plates. For a while, Gram's spicy burritos drove out serious conversation.

They lingered over dinner, but conversation was sparse. By the time Gram set a plate of cookies on the table, Dad was ready to talk about the accident again.

"Seemed like an awful long time between knowin'

Jeep would fall and the instant I hit the ground," Dad said.

"Like slow motion," Gram agreed. "At the heart of an emergency, time seems to click off one second at a time."

Dad rubbed the back of his neck. His brown eyes met Sam's. She didn't think she could have looked away if she'd wanted to.

"Here's the thing," Dad said. "In this sorta life, I could get hurt bad, even killed, any time."

Sam pushed back from the table. She didn't want to hear this, but Dad's eyes said she'd better not leave.

"I'm careful, sure," he said. "But total safety's impossible when you do what we do."

Why was Dad saying this? It was exactly what she tried *not* to think about.

"But job safety's not what I was frettin' about as Jeep was falling," Dad said with a half smile. "One sentence musta run through my head a dozen times. Know what it was? 'Oh shoot, I haven't taught her how to run the ranch.'"

The kitchen was quiet except for the coffeepot starting to perk.

Sam's gaze swung to Brynna, but her stepmother shook her head.

"You." Dad touched Sam's shoulder. "After I'm gone—"

"Dad, do we have to talk about this?" Sam felt

tears prick the corners of her eyes.

For most kids, this conversation would be an ugly "what if" situation. Not for Sam. She knew Dad could die. After all, Mom had.

"Starting tomorrow, I'm gonna start teaching you what it means to be a rancher," Dad told her.

Sam leaned back against her chair and felt as if she were shrinking. She hadn't even mastered life as a high school student, and now Dad wanted her to learn to take over the ranch.

Is that why Dad had let her go after the horses alone? Because he wanted her to know how to do things in case he died? That was way too much responsibility.

"Now, what else do you want to talk about?" Dad asked.

It was the opening Sam had been waiting for. She pushed aside her fear and started talking.

"Remember when I told you that Jen and I want to go on a campout?"

By the time Sam finished explaining Jen's plan to round up the strays as a Father's Day present, Brynna had gone upstairs to change out of her uniform and Gram was washing dishes.

Dad might have given her an outright "no" if Blaze hadn't jumped to his feet and begun sniffing at the bottom of the kitchen door.

"We'll see how this hound situation plays out, first," Dad said, distracted. "Just now, Blaze seems to think we have company."

Their visitor was Jed Kenworthy. Before he could even knock, Dad slipped outside.

"He doesn't want us in on whatever Jed's gonna tell him. It's got to be about Linc and the dogs, don't you think?" Sam asked Gram.

"You're probably right," Gram said. "But they've been doing this for years. Whenever there's a decision to be made about ranching, they stroll around, checking fences, looking over the stock, just generally summing things up while they talk. Sometimes they do it at our place and sometimes over at Gold Dust."

Sam wasn't the only one frustrated by Dad's solitary walk with Jed.

Once she came back downstairs in jeans and saw Dad gone, Brynna paced from the window over the sink to the one in the kitchen door, then back to the big window that wrapped the front of the house and gave the kitchen table its view.

Sam could see only darkness through each one of them, but Brynna kept peeking.

"They can have their conversation without me," Brynna said, as if convincing herself. "So I'm not going out there."

At last, Brynna busied herself with phone calls.

"I'm just giving our neighbors a heads-up," Brynna said as she dialed. "So they know that pack's on the prowl."

First, she called Three Ponies Ranch, but Jake

had already warned his family. They'd increased the hours each brother spent riding the range, keeping watch over their beef cattle.

Brynna's call worried Mrs. Allen. Just listening to one half of the conversation, Sam could tell Mrs. Allen feared the yapping of her Boston bulldogs, Imp and Angel, might attract the pack of hounds instead of discouraging them.

When Brynna hung up, she turned to Sam and Gram with a bemused smile.

"She's not the sort to just sit and worry, is she?" Brynna said. "Tomorrow, she's going into town to shop for dog repellent, and she's convinced there's something like a bug zapper, built strong enough for dogs."

"Where would you shop for things like that?" Sam asked, thinking of the campout.

"Don't ask me," Brynna said.

Gram chuckled. She and Mrs. Allen had recently rekindled an old friendship.

"Trudy Allen is a world-class shopper. If they exist this side of San Francisco, she'll find them."

When Dad returned to the house, Brynna was first to pounce on him with questions.

"Is Jed going to reinforce the kennel so those deerhounds stay home?" she asked.

"The kennel's sturdy enough to hold them. Linc's the problem."

"There's a surprise," Brynna said.

Gram cleared her throat and suppressed a smile as Brynna turned to Sam.

"That was rude of me. I don't mean to set a bad example, Sam."

"It's not like I wasn't already thinking the same thing," Sam said.

"Anyway," Dad continued, "Linc can't stay away from those dogs, but he can't control them, either. Still, Jed thinks Linc's a little shaken up by what happened today."

"As he should be," Brynna muttered.

"I'm banking on it," Dad said, as his attention swung to Sam. "Now, as for your campout, you can go if—"

Sam bounced out of her chair and jumped up and down, celebrating.

"If," Dad repeated, more loudly.

Sam sat down, but her mind was already spinning ahead. She and Jen would ride for two days, only stopping when they felt like it, sleeping out under the stars with two horses for company. It would be amazing, wonderful, cooler than anything she'd ever done.

But she'd better find out what followed Dad's *if*.

Sam settled back into her chair. All three adults watched her with amusement.

"If?" she said patiently, as if she hadn't just rejoiced like a five-year-old.

"You can go if, at the end of two days, I think you're gonna be useful out there."

"Okay," Sam said carefully.

"You'd be riding out to do work that should've been done right the first time."

So you'd better do it right this time. Sam heard Dad's hint.

"I'm not saying you two can't have some fun out of it, but you've got a lot to learn before you ride out— like ear-tagging a calf, and branding one."

Sam struggled to freeze her face. Hurting a calf, even for its own good, wasn't her idea of fun. But she couldn't let her city girl squeamishness show.

"Wyatt, end the child's suspense. How are you going to test her usefulness?" Gram asked.

"For the next couple days, you're gonna work for me as if you were on the verge of taking over as head honcho," Dad said.

Sam did not know what "head honcho" meant, exactly, but it must be someone in charge.

"I'll work *so* hard," Sam promised.

"Yes, you will," Dad agreed. "And in between the usual ranch chores, you're gonna polish your roping and learn to earmark our stock."

"You'll be glad we don't do it the old-fashioned way," Gram said. "Because one thing I know for sure is Samantha Anne Forster is too softhearted for cropping ears with a pocketknife."

Sam's hands gripped each other in her lap.

"But we don't do that," Sam affirmed.

"No, we don't," Dad said.

"And Jen's dad is okay with this, too?" Sam asked.

"Yep. He thinks most of the strays will belong to the Gold Dust Ranch, since it's their section you'll be riding. I'll send a branding iron along with you, but Jennifer will be marking Gold Dust stock more often than you'll be marking ours."

Sam's enthusiasm wavered. Earmarking cattle and branding them depended on roping. All her coordination fled when she tried to spin a lasso over her head, then fling it over anything.

Once, Pepper had rigged up a sawhorse with cow horns attached to it and shown her how he'd practiced when he'd decided to be a cowboy. It hadn't worked for her. No matter how often she sent her loop singing toward the mock cow, her rope had wobbled like limp spaghetti. She'd missed every time.

Now she had two days to change all that.

"Wyatt," Brynna said, "are you patient enough to teach Sam how to rope?"

"Of course." Dad sounded a bit insulted. "But I'm not going to do it."

"Dallas—" Gram began, shaking her head.

"Nope," Dad said. "Seems to me we've got a local expert who knows how to rope, but needs to polish his teaching skills before next week."

"Jake?" Sam squeaked her amazement.

Not after the way he'd shown off his roping skills today. No way.

She wet her lips and tried not to feel his rope

jerking tight, then dragging her off Ace and into the muddy lake. "Jake's going to teach me to rope?"

"That's right." Dad said it like a dare.

Sam rolled her eyes toward the kitchen ceiling. How much did she want to go on a campout with Jen? A lot. A whole lot.

Then she closed her eyes for an instant, hoping God had a sense of humor about little white lies before she met Dad's gaze.

"Great." She smiled so wide, her cheeks plumped up. "It'll be good for me and Jake to work together before the HARP girls come next week. I can hardly wait."

Chapter Nine ∾

Figuring she'd need every minute of sleep, Sam went to bed early, but excitement kept her awake.

On nights like this, she expected the Phantom to appear at the boundary of the ranch that had once been his home. But no matter how determinedly she listened, no faraway neigh floated to her. Staring from her bedroom window, she saw nothing but the La Charla's waving sheen as the river, lit by a half-moon, meandered around rocks and past cottonwood trees, heading for the bridge.

No horses, no deer, and no dangerous dogs showed themselves to her watchful eyes.

Sam climbed back into bed and pulled her covers up to her chin. She tried to get comfortable on her back, but in the dimness of her room, the uneven plaster of her ceiling looked like running white horses. Curled on her side, she watched her bedside clock until she was convinced it had slowed to half speed.

Maybe she was too hot. She tossed off her blanket and sheet. The sudden movement summoned her cat, Cougar. With a loud meow, he leaped onto her bed, flopped down, and began kneading her knees with pricking claws.

"If you want to cuddle," Sam told the young cat, "come up here."

Gently she closed her hands around Cougar's soft body and lifted him. Twisting wildly, he fought loose, jumped back to the floor, and skittered out her bedroom door.

"Be that way," Sam whispered after him, but now she was totally awake.

Sam sat up and checked the time again.

It was only ten o'clock. It was quiet downstairs, but she knew that when it was warm, Gram had trouble sleeping, too.

Dressing in lightweight sweats and tennis shoes, Sam listened for movement along the upstairs hallway. She heard Dad snoring as he did when he was really tired. But that was all.

Sam crept downstairs. The living room was dark. So was the kitchen, except for a small light over the stove.

She wasn't sneaking out. She just longed for the

warm privacy that wrapped around her when she sat at the riverside while everyone else was asleep.

Suddenly the kitchen grew even darker. Sam glanced toward the front kitchen window to see a cloud blocking the light of the moon. No big deal.

As she eased open the kitchen door, Sam heard a squeak that didn't come from the door hinge.

"Hello, dear."

Sam caught her breath. Just as she noticed movement to her left, she remembered Gram had moved her rocking chair to the front porch for such hot nights when she couldn't sleep.

"You didn't turn on the porch light," Sam gasped. "You surprised me."

Gram gave a low chuckle, then asked, "Did you hear Tempest's fussing all the way up in your room or are you just psychic, like most mothers?"

Sam laughed.

She wasn't exactly Tempest's mother. Dark Sunshine did a fine job of that, but Sam had been the first human to touch the black filly on the night she was born.

"What's she doing?" Sam asked.

Gram held her index finger to her lips, shushing Sam so that she could hear the patter of small hooves circling the barn corral.

Sam listened as Tempest ran around and around. Dirt crunched as she stopped, gave a squeal-snort, then continued her race with the night.

"I wonder why she's so restless?" Sam said.

"It's a warm night. The moon's playing peekaboo with the clouds and creating strange shadows. Plus, she takes lots of naps during the day," Gram suggested. "She's probably not sleepy."

Sam wanted to believe Gram, but an image of leaping, snapping dogs flashed into her mind.

"You don't think—"

"—something's wrong?" Gram finished for her, then shook her head. "I've been sitting here for close to an hour and Blaze is sleeping over by the bunkhouse. One of us would have noticed."

Sam trusted Gram's instincts. After all, Gram had grown up on River Bend Ranch. She could hear the difference between wind shaking a pinion pine and a cow brushing against that same pine to make it shiver.

"I'm going inside, but there's no reason you can't go down and check on your sassy little girl," Gram said.

When Sam kissed Gram's cheek, Gram's powdery scent banished the nightmare flashes of dogs. Sam sighed and smiled as she set out across the ranch yard toward the corral.

The saddle horses grazed at the far end of the ten-acre pasture. There were no snorts or nickers, even from Ace, as she passed by.

But Dark Sunshine heard her quiet steps and gave a low, inquiring whinny.

"Just me, Sunny."

The mare stamped, then rubbed against the corral fence.

Sunny sounded peaceful tonight. Sam didn't think the mare would try to push past her as she entered the corral. Just the same, Sam decided to go into the barn and through the stall that opened into the corral. Sunny's mustang heart still longed for the open range.

When she first stepped into the corral, Sam was surprised by the buckskin's greeting. Sunny trotted to meet her, then rubbed her forelock against Sam's chest so hard that she stumbled back a step.

"What are you girls doing tonight?"

The mustang's ears twitched at the puff of Sam's human breath, but she didn't seem to mind. Cautiously and gently, Sam slipped her fingers beneath Sunny's black mane and stroked her buckskin neck.

Tempest raised her forefeet off the ground a few inches and gave a tiny snort. Abruptly Sunny's head swung to consider her foal.

"You're just amazed anyone would want to pet your mom instead of you, aren't you?" Sam asked the filly.

Tempest answered by slipping past her mother to rub her muzzle on Sam's cheek.

"Is that a kiss, pretty girl?" Sam crooned to the filly.

Tempest's brown eyes caught the faint light from the stars overhead. She didn't step away when Sam gently hugged her neck.

Gratitude glowed in Sam's heart. No one had a better life than she did.

"You're soft as velvet," Sam told the filly, but when Tempest suddenly stiffened against her, she knew why.

Something had moved on the hillside.

Sunny stared into the darkness.

Inch by inch, Sam lifted her arms from Tempest and strained her eyes until they felt hot from trying to see beyond the fence.

While Sam searched the night, Tempest rocketed into her circling gallop once more.

Was it a survival response? Generations of mustangs had run from sounds in the night. Maybe Tempest did the same.

Once, on the stormy night of Tempest's birth, the Phantom had descended the path from the ridge. But Sam really didn't think he'd do it again. For his own safety, she had whirled her arms and yelled to drive him away.

But *something* was up there now.

And Gram had gone back into the house.

Whatever it was, Sam knew she was out here with it alone.

Dark Sunshine gave a snort of recognition. She saw whatever it was and moved to confront it.

The next time Tempest raced past, Sunny clacked her teeth in warning. Tempest slid to a stop and scampered a few steps off. Out of reach, she bucked in defiance. Only when Sunny threatened a real bite did Tempest tuck close to her mother's body.

There! The dark shape was no creation of moonshine and shadows. It was much larger than a dog; Sam was certain it was a horse.

Suddenly Sam saw him.

The mustang stood halfway down the ridge, just where the Phantom had watched on that stormy night. In profile his mane moved like a flame. His head was dished like a hot-blooded Arabian. His legs were long and sculpted for speed. It must be the Phantom.

But then, as the clouds parted, Sam saw that the wild horse was black.

"New Moon," she whispered.

Sunny saw him, too, and issued a ringing neigh. Sam stumbled as the buckskin's shoulder grazed her, but she got her hands down in time to catch herself and push back up to her feet.

Sunny raced toward the far fence, veered right just before colliding with it, then whirled back to challenge the stallion.

He answered with a coaxing nicker. Sam didn't have to be a horse to understand that New Moon had just told Sunny not to be so mean.

Sam froze. If the breeze shifted, Moon would catch her scent and probably gallop away. He had no bond with her as the Phantom did.

Dark Sunshine had drawn him to River Bend

Ranch, but she wasn't interested in eloping. Did she remember him as a young upstart who'd been banished from the Phantom's band?

Sam saw no movement behind the young stallion. Linc had claimed he'd seen a black stallion with two fine mares, but Moon seemed to be alone. If Moon didn't yet have a herd of his own, he might be here to start one.

Moon's single step forward crossed an invisible boundary. Sunny bolted forward against the fence, then wheeled and lashed out with her heels.

Sam winced. Sunny was only trying to drive Moon away, but nothing good could come out of splintering that fence.

What if the stallion jumped over the lower rails and drove her out with hooves and teeth? Sunny might change her mind and go with him. At the very least, Sam knew she'd be responsible for fixing the broken fence rails.

Then Tempest whinnied and changed everything.

Moon's voice rang in a commanding neigh. Sunny swerved away from the fence, head lowered.

Oh no, Sam thought. The buckskin mare had made a submissive move no stallion could miss.

"Sunny, no!" Sam shouted. All three horses startled as if she'd wakened them from a dream.

In a blur of black, Moon shied, then leaped up the hillside.

Tempest wanted to follow.

Sam's heart fell as she realized the filly would have gone if she could have.

Tempest shouldered past Sunny and resumed her reckless race around the corral.

The front porch light flashed on in time to show Tempest running. Her head shook from side to side in frustration. More than anything, she wanted to chase after Moon and follow her half brother back to the open range.

Chapter Ten ❧

ℋooves pounded across the ten-acre pasture.

The screen door slammed open and light feet crossed the wooden porch.

The only thing missing from this night alarm was the sound of Blaze barking.

"Was it the Phantom?" Brynna called as she hurried across the ranch yard, tying the sash on her red bathrobe.

Sam was astounded to see her. The last time there'd been a commotion like this, Dad had come running with a rifle.

Sam didn't have an instant to answer before she flattened herself against the corral fence. Dark Sunshine used nips to drive Tempest into the barn.

The mare was angry. No way did Sam want to get between her and Tempest.

At last the filly's head drooped in weariness and she obeyed. They trotted into the barn, Sunny still scolding with a clack of her teeth.

Sam followed the horses, shot the stall bolt behind them, then let herself out of the corral gate to meet Brynna.

"I can't believe Dad's not right behind you," Sam said.

"I pulled rank and told him I was the wild horse expert." Brynna pushed her loose hair away from her face.

"How did you know it was a—I mean, what you asked before—it wasn't the Phantom. It was Moon, the black . . ." Sam tried not to sputter, but thoughts pelted through her mind faster than her tongue could put them in order.

Finally, Sam shook her head and asked, "How did you know it wasn't the dogs?"

"Catch your breath," Brynna said, resting one hand on Sam's shoulder. "Your Dad and I both knew, because we heard the stallion. He was romancing the mare, not trying to drive off wild dogs."

That was what she'd guessed, but Sam still couldn't believe Dad hadn't come running. Brynna must have recognized her amazement.

"My claim to be the wild horse expert never would have worked if I hadn't beaten him down the stairs," Brynna conceded. "And the only reason I could do *that* was the stiffness from his fall. Wyatt's in a little pain." Brynna nodded with certainty. "Not that he'll admit it, but bruises don't lie."

"He's not hurt badly, is he?" Sam asked.

"Do you think your Gram and I would let him play the tough guy if he needed to see a doctor?"

"Not really . . ." Sam began.

"Not a chance." Brynna crossed her arms and lifted her chin.

The night seemed to settle around them, and both Brynna and Sam looked toward the hillside.

"It was Moon," Sam said.

Brynna took a deep breath, and her arms fell to her sides. "We haven't seen him for a while."

Last fall in Arroyo Azul, Sam and Brynna had seen the young stallion battle his sire.

The challenge had been bloody and brief. The young stallion had courage but little experience. He had speed and stamina, but his sire had strength and strategy. New Moon had fled the fight and remained at Aspen Creek with only a half-grown cougar for company.

"Did he have any mares with him?" Brynna asked.

"I didn't see any," Sam said. She was about to tell Brynna what Linc had said, when she remembered a sighting of her own. "But earlier today I saw some horses, just barely," she admitted, recalling her stranding in the lake on Ace. "Mostly what I saw was dust, but that's when I heard those hounds baying for the first time. That dust cloud on the hill might have been Moon with a couple of mares."

"Last fall Jake saw him with a mare, didn't he?"

Sam considered her stepmother with admiration. When it came to wild horses, Brynna didn't miss much.

"He told me he saw Moon with a red mare," Sam said. "The Phantom still has two blood bays in his band, but I remember a red chestnut. . . . Do you think he could have stolen her from the Phantom? The way they were fighting, I can't believe Moon got away with it."

"The Phantom might have let her go. The daughters of a herd stallion are supposed to be taken into another band."

Sam nodded. Even at this time of night, Brynna could sound like a biologist.

"In fact, there's something else we need to talk about."

Sam's trouble radar flashed on.

Something we need to talk about rarely meant something good.

"Okay," Sam said.

"Now that Sunny and Tempest are locked in for the night, let's have a cup of tea before we settle down, too."

"Sounds good," Sam said, though she was pretty sure she was hours from settling down.

Moon's appearance and Tempest's reaction to him had Sam's mind darting all over the place. And what did Brynna want to discuss?

As she stepped onto the porch, Sam glanced back over her shoulder toward the bunkhouse. Usually this kind of excitement had Blaze bouncing around her ankles, but he was nowhere to be seen.

Five minutes later, Brynna clutched the handles of two mugs of mint tea in one hand and a honeypot in the other as she came to the kitchen table.

Sam drizzled a stream of honey into her tea, but she was watching Brynna from beneath lowered eyelashes. Absently, her stepmother braided her hair, reached the bottom of the plait and discovered she had nothing to bind it, then tossed it back over her shoulder.

Something was making Brynna uneasy. She pushed her mug aside, rested her elbows on the kitchen table, and looked into Sam's eyes.

"There's a fact of mustang life that's not pretty."

Sam squared her shoulders. Did this have to do with the constant range battle between cattle ranchers and wild horses? Was Brynna, as a Bureau of Land Management employee, caught in the middle again?

"And since you'll be out alone in wild horse

country for a couple days," Brynna continued, "you should know about it."

She already knew about the food rivalry between cattle and horses. What could Brynna be talking about?

Brynna knew Sam had loved horses forever. She'd read books about them and listened in on cowboys talking of horses for most of her fourteen years.

Clearly, though, Brynna thought she was about to reveal something shocking.

"I'm ready," Sam encouraged her.

"When stallions fight, they prove more than their dominance. They prove their right to father the next generation of colts."

"I know," Sam said. "I was just thinking about that. Moon lost that fight we saw in Arroyo Azul because the Phantom was stronger and smarter."

"Right," Brynna said. "So nothing really changed in the Phantom's herd, but it might have. If Moon had won, he would have been the new boss at a time when mares were already in foal to the Phantom."

"So?"

"So . . ." Brynna stretched the word out a little longer than usual. "The new stallion would have won the right to father the next generation."

Sam knew horses were smart, but what Brynna was saying seemed far-fetched even to her.

"Would Moon actually know that?"

"Somehow they seem to," Brynna said. "And that's not horse-lover talk, that's science."

Sam took a gulp of tea and waited.

"Sometimes the victorious stallion doesn't want the other stallion's foals around. He'll be rough with the mares or run them too fast, too far, causing so much stress, the mares don't give birth to the foals they're carrying."

Sam stayed quiet, but she felt a wave of relief.

The Phantom's foals had already been born. The leggy colts and fillies were several months old. In the unlikely event that another stallion won against the Phantom, his foals should be safe.

"This time of the year," Brynna went on, "it can get even uglier."

"How?" Sam said impatiently. If Brynna had bad news, why didn't she just spit it out? "I'm not a little kid, you know. Just tell me."

"A conquering stallion might kill the foals that aren't his."

Without meaning to, Sam closed her eyes. She opened them just as quickly.

"I think maybe Jake told me that," Sam said. "But he doesn't like mustangs as much as I do. I thought he was exaggerating."

"He's not. Biologists used to think it was just an old cowboy story, but now there's research to prove it."

Sam stared into her empty mug.

Stallions wouldn't kill foals out of spite or jealousy. It was Nature's way of ensuring only the strong horses reproduced. But the *why* wouldn't matter to the babies or their mothers.

Distress showed in her expression, Sam guessed, because Brynna said, "It helps me to remember that wild horses wouldn't have survived years full of snowstorms, droughts, and predators if the herds hadn't been strong.

"Wild animals didn't need us until we started messing with their environment, bringing in highways and buildings and stuff." Brynna shrugged. "It's too late to go back, I guess, but there are some things they'll do with or without our interference. This is one of them."

As she tried to process all Brynna had said, Sam felt tired. Not sleepy, exactly, but exhausted.

"So," she managed, "you think I might see another stallion trying to kill the Phantom's foals?"

"No. No stallion out there can match him—"

Sam smiled, despite the somber topic. Her colt Blackie had grown up to be a king of wild horses.

"—and that's one reason I released him after he was brought in that day, last year. He's an amazing example of what mustangs can be. He's improving the herds' bloodlines. But the Phantom steals mares from other stallions."

Brynna stared at her meaningfully.

Finally, Sam understood. She held her breath until her lungs burned beneath her ribs.

"Oh," was the only word she could manage.

Brynna was saying the Phantom might be a killer.

Chapter Eleven ❧

In the kitchen's midnight quiet, the refrigerator hummed. The cooling kettle pinged on the stove. Bedsprings creaked upstairs.

"But the Phantom might *not* kill foals, even if they belong to other stallions," Sam said.

"You're right. It's not a rule in wild horse behavior," Brynna agreed. "And if he did, it's unlikely you'd see it. But if you do, I want you to understand."

And not blame him for it, Brynna's tone implied, but her stepmother didn't know Sam had been to the Phantom's secret valley and watched the wild horses in their family group. Except for a few territorial squeals and kicks, it had seemed so peaceful. And when she'd seen the Phantom with a new mare—like Golden

Rose, the Kenworthys' lost palomino—she hadn't seen any violence.

Those two thoughts made her feel better. After all, even a biologist like Brynna had to admit not all stallions acted the same.

Footsteps came down the stairs. Even at a slow, uneven pace, Sam recognized Dad's approach. He didn't come into the kitchen, though; he just called quietly from the stairs.

"Everything all right in there?"

"Fine," Brynna answered.

There was a moment of silence in which Sam felt Dad's impatience to know what was going on.

"You two down here eating up dinner leftovers?" Dad asked.

Sam's stomach wobbled at the thought of the red chili burritos. Her conversation with Brynna had squashed her late-night appetite.

"We're just having a cup of tea," Sam said.

She and Brynna smiled. Dad thought sipping tea was like drinking hot water. He sure wouldn't come in to join them.

"We'll be up in a minute, Wyatt."

"Okay, then," Dad said. "Sweet dreams."

Oh yeah, Sam thought as she stood and rinsed her mug out at the sink. *Sweet dreams*.

Despite her misgivings, Sam slept like a stone.

It was a good thing. Although he moved stiffly,

Dad worked harder than usual and expected Sam to keep up.

Even before they left the house at dawn, Dad served up a lecture with her breakfast.

"First thing you need to know is, ranchers farm, but farmers don't ranch."

Was that a riddle?

Sam didn't ask what he meant, but she stopped chewing and only recommenced as Dad explained.

"We raise hay, but there's no surplus. We raise it to feed our own stock. And all the agricultural kinda work we do—tending irrigation systems, fixing the baler, fussing over machinery—is just time robbed from our work with the cattle. Ross enjoys working on vehicles, so we're lucky. But if you watch Pepper, you'll see how he feels the difference between those chores."

Right away, Sam knew what Dad was talking about.

"His hats," Sam said, suddenly.

"That's right," Dad said. "He wears his Cat hat— the cap he got from the Caterpillar Tractor salesman—when he's not on horseback. . . ."

"And his Stetson when he is," Sam finished for him.

"Now, a real buckaroo," Dad said, "and there are still some around—Nevada being one of the last open-range states where not all cattle are fattened in crowded pens—won't do the sort of work I ask of Pepper and Ross. Dallas, for instance," Dad said, smiling. "Why, if I asked him to tinker with the engine on a tractor, he'd just pick up his saddle and head on down the road."

Sam laughed, but she could picture the white-haired, bowlegged foreman doing just that.

After they walked outside together and Dad told her what he expected, Sam decided she had the nature of a buckaroo, too.

"First thing you're gonna do is clean this whole yard," Dad said.

What? She'd rather work double hours, even triple, with cattle and horses.

"Hey, you know what?" Sam blurted. "I don't need to, because just last week the HARP girls picked up stuff. It doesn't need to be done again already."

"I'll show you where you're wrong."

Dad motioned Sam to come along with him toward their flock of Rhode Island Red hens. Chirring and scratching, the hens watched them with suspicious yellow eyes.

Dad couldn't mean the hens were messing things up, could he?

He pointed at the smallest of the rust-red hens. As Sam and Dad watched, the little hen hopped, flapped her wings, then tipped over.

"Is she injured?" Sam asked.

"Keep watching," Dad said.

Making a low complaining sound, the hen fluttered upright, strutted along awkwardly with the rest of her flock, then fell again.

This time she beat her wings wildly, causing the others to cackle, scatter, and leave her all alone.

"What's wrong with her?" Sam wanted to help, but she couldn't see how to do it.

"Guess if you're the rancher and you want to keep having eggs for breakfast, you'd better figure that out."

Sam watched the little hen jostle with the others for room in Gram's garden.

Gram must have opened the gate to her rabbit-proof fence earlier, because the hens were already pecking and scratching.

Gram complained about cut worms and grass-hoppers and other insect invaders that couldn't be fenced out, but she didn't like spraying poison to protect her crops.

It looked like the insects that were pests to Gram were delicious breakfast treats for the hens.

But that didn't solve the mystery of the falling fowl, so Sam moved closer.

The little hen pecked, but she didn't scratch in the dirt. Maybe something was wrong with her feet.

Now that the hens were penned on three sides, it should be easy to catch and examine the one that kept tipping over.

It wasn't as easy as it looked.

As Sam maneuvered her boots between sprouting

cucumbers, tomatoes, and onions, the hens skittered among the plants, digging in their delicate claws like the spikes of track shoes, moving out of reach.

She got close enough to see what was wrong with the hen, though. A white string, like the ones pulled loose to open a sack of feed, was wound around the hen's legs like a hobble.

"All I have to do is take it off," Sam muttered. Then, closing in behind the hen, she grabbed. "Gotcha."

She'd been pecked a few times as she reached under the feathers of a setting hen for an egg, so she wasn't afraid of the hen's sharp beak or the menace in her tiny yellow eyes. In fact, for just a second, the hen's downy softness was wonderful to hold.

Then, wings flapped wildly. The panicked hen struggled and defended herself with beak and claws.

"Ow, ow, ow!" Sam finally held the hen with one arm, blinking against the wings in her face as she leaned close to see how to untangle the string.

At last, Sam got it loose.

"Go, already," she said, setting the hen on the ground.

With an insulted cluck, the chicken hurried off to look for bugs, leaving Sam to inspect her long red scratches.

"Not too grateful, is she?" Dad said, laughing, when Sam finally returned to where he stood near the barn.

"No," Sam grumbled. "But I got this." She presented Dad with the string. "That's what was making her trip."

"Now where do you suppose that came from?" Dad asked, and Sam explained her feed sack theory.

"Good eye," he congratulated her. Then, before she could feel proud, he asked, "What are you gonna do about it?"

"I think she's okay," Sam said, looking back at the hen. Now that she was feasting alongside her sisters, Sam couldn't tell the hen from the others.

"For now," Dad said. "But there's a lot of little trash around this yard that could hurt her or the other animals."

This wasn't what most people thought of as ranching, Sam thought.

She spent two hours picking up sticks and branches that had blown down in the summer wind. She raked up leaves, weeds, little scraps of paper, and more bits of string.

With her sweatshirt tied around her waist, she was deciding whether to return to the house and change into shorts when Dad pointed out empty feed sacks that had accumulated, and told her they should be burned.

Dad didn't have to tell her to be careful.

She'd had close encounters with both snakes and fires. Each time she picked up anything that could hide a snake, she moved gingerly. She cleared a huge space before starting the fire.

Sam was wiping her forehead with the back of her hand and standing guard over the fire when Dad asked, "Makes a smoky fire, doesn't it?"

Sam gave him a sideways glance. "Yeah," she agreed.

"Once you're done, go ahead and break for lunch. After that, Jake should be here. Once you've had some practice with the rope, we'll talk about branding."

"Okay," Sam said. She watched Dad walk toward the barn and wondered if he really expected her to squeeze all that into a single day.

Soon Dad released Sunny and Tempest into the barn corral. *I can do that*, Sam thought. When she saw him checking the water troughs and spreading something on a fence rail where Sunny had been cribbing, chewing out of boredom or nerves, Sam knew she could do that, too.

But Sam didn't pout.

I can put up with anything for a couple days of freedom.

While she poked at the last burning scrap of gunnysack, Sam heard Sunny trotting around the barn pen.

Was the mare remembering last night?

Sam hoped she'd scared Moon enough that he wouldn't return. If he had mares of his own, he probably wouldn't risk the threat of humans. But if he was alone, he might decide Sunny, Strawberry, or Penny would relish an escape.

And what about Tempest?

Would he welcome her into his band? Or punish her for being the Phantom's daughter?

Sam couldn't help remembering what Brynna had told her about the way rival stallions treated each other's foals.

She tried to block the image of Moon kicking the black filly.

Don't think that, she ordered her brain.

It didn't help.

Memories of her own skull's collision with a hoof rushed over her. Sam recalled an impact so strong it lifted her head and shoulders from the dirt. Then dizziness had come and with it the sound of hooves moving away, growing fainter, as Jake shouted her name.

Sam shook her head, almost expecting it to hurt. It didn't, of course, but it reminded her that her head injury had been an accident. Blackie, her own hand-raised colt who'd grown up to be the Phantom, had run away and his hoof had just happened to graze her head. A kick that was aimed and intentional would be much worse.

And Tempest was so small.

As she stared into the twists of orange flame, Sam heard a gate latch clank behind her.

Come to think of it, the sound of metal on metal had been going on for a while. Sam turned to see Ace at the gate of the ten-acre pasture.

He must be itchy, because it looked like he was scratching his chin on the wooden fence. She'd started to look away when she realized the bay mustang was lipping the lock.

"Hey!" she shouted. Ace backed away from the fence, but when she didn't leave the fire to come after him, he lowered his head and set to work on the lock again.

It wasn't the first time Ace had pulled this trick. Sam remembered a day when Karla Starr, an unscrupulous rodeo contractor, had been at the ranch sizing up Popcorn as a bucking horse.

Ace had come ambling up to Sam, having somehow released himself from his stall. He'd known how to open that latch. And just the other day, all the saddle horses had escaped. That couldn't be a coincidence.

Sam used her rake to scatter the ashes of the fire. It wasn't likely to burn out of control, but she was taking no chances.

She dropped the rake and ran toward the pasture. Throwing his head high, eyes rolling in mock terror, Ace backed away from the gate again.

"You won't fake me out this time," Sam said.

The clever gelding must have understood, because he bolted into a run, swiveling his heels toward the fence.

"At least they didn't escape," Sam told Dad when he came up to find her checking the lock.

"They might have gone farther this time," Dad said.

Sam nodded. With Jake on his way here for

roping lessons, she wouldn't have had time to catch the horses and do everything that Dad wanted done.

"So what are you gonna do about it?"

"Do?" Sam asked.

It was the second time Dad had asked the question this morning. Of course, she'd understood something had to be done to keep the hobbled hen from becoming easy prey for a coyote. But this was harder.

"I caught Ace in time and yelled at him. I don't think —"

Liar, Sam silently interrupted herself. Catching Ace in the act of picking the lock on the gate wouldn't stop him from another attempt, and she knew it.

The next time Ace was restless and bored, he'd try again.

Stalling because she didn't know what to do, Sam glanced over at the smoldering ashes.

"Is that going to be okay?" she asked.

Dad gave an infuriating shrug. Sam gave a too-loud sigh, then stalked back to the ashes.

It looked okay to her, and Dad had said Gram had some garden use for cold ashes.

What was it?

Sam was trying to remember, when the lock clinked again.

"Fire's out," Sam said as she jogged back. "Ace, stop that!"

She clapped her hands to drive him back. He

retreated a few steps, swished his tail lazily, and nickered. He wasn't a bit frightened by her warning. He was having fun.

Sam considered the bolt on the gate. "I could padlock it," she said, eyes checking with Dad.

"You could," he agreed. "But then you'd need a key to let the horses out."

That would be stupid. If she'd needed a key to release the saddle horses on the night of the fire—

What about a combination lock? No way, that would have been even worse. She couldn't even remember numbers when she was sitting in a quiet classroom. With a fire raging behind her, she would be useless to the horses.

"Help," she said, finally.

Dad took pity on her frustration. He showed her how to unscrew the lock, chip away at the wood, and recess the lock so that it wasn't hard to open with fingers, but should be impossible for horse lips.

She worked alone, with only Ace for a supervisor.

Half an hour later, when she was finished, the gelding nuzzled her hair.

"You think you're so cute," Sam said as sweat dripped from her forehead into one eye.

Of course, Ace *was* cute. And clever. And more loyal and tolerant than any human.

Even before she rubbed the eye that was stinging from sweat, Sam reached a hand up to touch the muzzle Ace pressed against her ear.

Ace took a step backward, shook his head, and flipped his forelock clear of his white star.

Friends? he seemed to be asking.

Sam laughed. Tired and cranky as she was, she couldn't stay mad.

Chapter Twelve ⌘

Wondering if she'd ever been so tired, Sam sucked the index finger she'd just pulled a sliver of wood from.

Just then, she heard the clop of hooves and saw Jake riding across the bridge.

She took a deep breath.

Am I up for this?

Of all the ranch skills she'd attempted so far, roping was hardest. Every single time she'd tried, she'd failed. And yet, if she planned to go out with Jen and actually earmark and brand calves, she'd have to learn.

Jake rode Chocolate Chip. The dark brown Quarter Horse belonged to Jake's brother Bryan.

Though Chip was as muscled and quick as Witch, he had a better temperament.

Jake led a half-grown calf.

Yep, Sam thought, that meant she was about to receive roping lessons, whether she wanted them or not.

She wouldn't give up. She *couldn't* give up.

So why was she leaning against a post, slowly sliding down until she sat cross-legged with her back against the fence?

When Jake rode right up to where she sat, Sam stared at Chip's hooves.

Jake's words tumbled down from overhead.

"Hey Brat, you get into a wrestlin' match with a wildcat?"

Sam raised one arm and inspected her chicken scratches. They'd bled a little. Her hands were scuffed and scraped, too, from learning to use the chisel on the fence.

She tried to think back as far as dawn, and realized she hadn't brushed her hair this morning, either.

If Jake wanted to tease her now, she didn't have the energy to fight back.

"No wildcats." Sam stifled a yawn and looked up past Chip's knees and chest to Jake, who was sitting in the saddle. "Just a huffy hen and an out-of-control tool."

Jake smiled and Sam remembered why, when she was a little kid, she'd thought Jake had mustang eyes.

Brown and lively, they shone from the shade of his hat brim, their expression just as mischievous as a wild horse peering from behind his tangled forelock.

"Have you eaten?" Jake asked.

"Yeah, scrambled eggs," she muttered. "Dad pretty much told me if I ever wanted them again I had to fix that monster hen."

"I meant lunch."

How long ago had Dad said she could break for lunch? Sam had no idea.

"I'm not really hungry," she said, though after she'd told Jake what she'd done all day, she was amazed she wasn't famished.

"We can't start till you have some water, at least," Jake said, and when he walked her to the kitchen, Gram took over.

After she'd had a tuna sandwich, chips, and three glasses of lemonade, Sam felt as if she'd clicked on a light switch in her brain.

"You brought a calf," Sam said as she and Jake walked back outside.

"I wondered what that was, following me."

"Be serious," Sam said. "Shouldn't we start by roping a stump or something?"

"You've done that already."

"I've tried," Sam corrected him.

"Well, today you're gonna try catching Dewey. He's my mom's pet orphan and she thinks he looks like Thomas Dewey," Jake explained.

"Who?"

"The guy who was supposed to beat some other guy for president a long time ago." Jake shrugged as if she shouldn't blame him for a name given by his history teacher mom. "I don't know, Sam, but he's the perfect calf for ropin' practice. You'll see."

Sam bit her lip. There wasn't much of a chance she'd actually get a loop around a moving neck if she couldn't catch a stationary object. Still, she knew what would happen if she did.

Ace would slide to a stop and, if she did her part, the rope would strain in a straight line from her hand to the calf's neck. The calf wouldn't know until it hit the end of the rope and was jerked off its feet that it had been caught.

"His poor little neck," Sam said, knowing it was a totally unrancherlike comment.

"You're going to be heeling him," Jake corrected. "Putting a loop around his back legs is safer for the calf. And with just you and Jen working, it'll be more efficient."

Sam felt a little relieved.

"And you won't hurt him," Jake promised. "Dewey's different than other calves. Soon as he feels the rope, he flops down, like he wants his belly rubbed. Drives ropin' horses crazy. When Dewey pulled it with Witch, she wanted to rush up and bite him. That's why I rode Chip."

Sam looked down at the ground between her boots. If she planned to live on a ranch, if she wanted to be the partner Dad expected, she didn't have much choice.

"I'll try," Sam said.

"'Course you will," Jake said. "Do you want to use my rope?"

"Dad gave me one. I'm just awful with it."

"Show me," he said. "Spin it over your head," he said, as if it were just a first step instead of an impossibility. "Don't throw it at anything."

"Okay," she said. "Here goes."

She really tried, but the loop flopped like a dead flower.

"Faster," Jake suggested, but when Sam spun her wrist with more speed, Jake just stepped out of range.

"Hmph," he said, sounding puzzled.

"See? It's hopeless," Sam said.

Jake shook his head. "If wild colts can learn barrel racin', something that makes no sense to 'em, you can learn to rope."

"You might be right," Sam said. Trust Jake to use a horse example that actually gave her hope.

And it turned out he was right.

Somehow, when Jake wrapped his fingers around hers on the lariat, modeling the correct hand position before she raised it over her head, roping became possible.

It took a while to get the speed and balance right,

but the rope no longer felt too fat or too thin in her fingers. Now it felt just right.

Jake never took his eyes from her. He watched, telling her when the diameter of her loop reached six to eight inches.

When her wrist began to ache, she stopped and rubbed it.

"Keep goin'," Jake said.

"My wrist hurts and my mind is spinning faster than my loop," she told him.

"Don't think," he said, as if it was an obvious mistake. "Do what I do."

Jake set an example with his own rope, spinning the loop clockwise at a smooth, hypnotic pace.

Sam kept her eyes on Jake, and gradually the movement began to feel natural, almost graceful.

"You're getting it," Jake said as if he'd never doubted she would, and Sam kept spinning.

He let his loop fall when she'd spun the rope over her head for a full three minutes.

"You're a wizard," Sam told him. She didn't have a single qualm left about Jake's ability to teach the HARP girls.

"You ain't caught anything yet," he snorted, pulling in his rope and recoiling it. "What I taught ya so far's not good for nothing."

Sam couldn't understand why Jake acted ignorant when she complimented him, but she let it go as he talked her through the next few steps.

As Jake swung into Chip's saddle, the brown gelding danced with excitement.

Dewey was tied to the hitching post, switching his tail and looking bored.

"You're gonna use an underhand flick to toss the loop. Like this." He sent the rope out, then pulled it back. "Do it."

"But I'm just standing here," Sam protested.

"Like this." He repeated the action.

"But I'm not roping anything."

"Could ya just trust me on this and pretend?" Jake asked.

Sam guessed that was fair. An hour ago, she hadn't been able to spin the rope over her head and now she could.

"Okay, I'm roping an air cow," Sam said.

"Not unless you point your index finger," Jake said, as she made a miserable attempt. "Try it again. There," he said as she threw, pulled back her rope, and threw again. "Better, lots better. When you get mounted and try this, remember that even though your brain wants to aim the rope right at Dewey, you can't. The calf's running—"

"But Jake, I mess up when it's *not* running. When it's not even alive."

"Not this time," he told her. "This time, you're gonna aim ahead of the calf, cause if you aim where he is, Dewey'll be gone by the time the rope gets there."

It all made sense, and Jake claimed she was getting better. And then he told her to saddle Ace.

"But wait, I still haven't roped anything."

"Don't worry so much," Jake said as he pulled his own rope in, coiled it in a loop, and fastened it to his saddle.

"I expect you'll miss a few times, but then Ace will get you in position and—piece of cake."

At last, with Dad's help, they moved Dewey to the barn corral.

Still spinning the rope over her head, Sam got ready as Dad gave Dewey a head start.

"Heel kick," Jake shouted. "Go!"

Sam jerked her boot heels back, but Ace was already springing after the calf.

Around and around, her hand spun in a small circle.

The loop stayed up!

Aim ahead of the calf. The pounding of Ace's hooves surrounded Jake's lessons. *Where Dewey will be, not where he is.*

Not yet.

Sam shifted as Ace cornered, staying after the calf but not too close.

The loop was still up.

Not yet.

There! Her arm darted forward and the loop floated. As if by remote control, it snagged the calf's hind legs. Just as it began to tighten, Dewey flopped on his side.

Ace slid to a stop, pulling the calf back a full yard.

"Whoa!" Sam shouted, but Ace ignored her.

"It's okay," Jake shouted. "You'd have to drag him to the fire for branding, anyway. Ace is practicin', too."

Sam leaned forward. She patted Ace's shoulder as she'd seen Dad do. Like magic, Ace took a step and let his head hang down a bit.

Jake walked forward, leaned down, and stroked Dewey's belly.

"Now, your normal calf will be fighting and trying to get up at this point." Jake spread the loop and removed it from Dewey's hind legs.

Then Jake faced Sam with a grin.

"Not bad," he said.

Ace pranced and Sam turned him in a circle until she came back around to face Jake.

"I had a good teacher," she told him.

"We all know that's not true," Jake grumped.

But it *was* true. All at once Sam remembered that Jake had taught her to gentle Blackie. And that bond had lasted.

Four out of six times, Sam made successful catches. Then, Jake said it was time to stop.

"You let Jen be the mugger," Jake said.

"The—?" Sam was sure her face looked as blank as her brain felt.

"Someone's gotta wrestle most calves down," Jake explained, then looked thoughtful. "In fact, I

wouldn't be surprised if Jen has you do all the vaccinating, branding, and marking, while she holds the
calf still."

"I'm as strong as she is," Sam protested, though
her mind was still weighing which was worse: burning a calf with a hot iron, or holding it down so Jen
could.

Vaccinating? Sam knew calves had to get shots,
just like kids did when they went to the doctor's
office. But she had no idea how to give a vaccination.

It was four o'clock by the time Sam swung down
from the saddle, loosened Ace's cinch, and slid the
saddle from his back.

She gasped at the stab of soreness that ran from
her right inner arm to her fingertips.

Jake, walking away from a ground-tied Chip,
was tightening the rawhide thong around his black
hair.

"Hurts, don't it?" he asked. "You use those same
roping muscles for lifting that saddle off and on."

"I'm okay," Sam said, but the pain had arced like
fire through her surprised arms and down her torso.

Sam walked Ace around to cool him, then
brushed his sweaty coat dry.

Jake walked around aimlessly, never getting
more than a few yards away.

Even Ace noticed Jake's restlessness, and he
pointed it out to Sam by tipping his ears in Jake's
direction.

"What?" Sam demanded finally, but Jake only shrugged. "I always knew someday you'd use up your supply of words," she grumbled just loudly enough for him to hear. "I guess that's why you're so stingy with them."

Sam rubbed her forehead.

That was a mistake. Not only did bits of dirt fall into her eyes, but the blisters on her palms stung with salt from her sweaty brow.

Who would have guessed ranching was so much work and hurt so much?

A whistle sounded near the bunkhouse. Dallas tilted his head to look under the porch, then he kept moving with a bowlegged sway.

Sam figured her revelation about hard work and ranching probably wouldn't surprise Dallas. Or Dad.

"When you do rope a range calf," Jake said, suddenly, "be careful. They're wild as deer."

Jake looked around for Dad. Did Jake think he'd be rescued from giving her this lecture, or did he want Dad to back him up?

"I'll be careful." Sam tried to make her tone soothing, but Jake decided she was minimizing what he'd said.

"This is no joke." Jake shook his finger so near her face, Sam would have grabbed it, if he hadn't looked truly worried. "Watch out for those little hooves. They'll cut you like a butcher knife."

"Okay."

"And some of those calves are only a month old. They've never seen a human. They're scared of you to begin with. How much more are they gonna be likin' you after you pierce their ears and brand 'em with a white-hot iron?"

Sam swallowed hard.

"What I'm sayin'—"

"I hear what you're saying," she assured him, and this time he believed her.

"Okay. Just let Jen do the close work. She's more experienced."

Sam nodded.

"Still," Jake said. "I guess you gotta learn some-time."

Logic suddenly elbowed Sam's fear aside.

"Hey, how old were you when you started doing this stuff?" she asked.

"Old enough."

Jake crossed his arms and Sam did the same so quickly, she might have been his reflection.

"Dad said there's only one way to learn to be a buckaroo," Sam reminded him.

"The hard way," Jake said. "Yeah, I know."

Since that was as good an ending as this conversation would ever have, Sam started to squat down to grab the hoof-pick. She sucked in her breath and put one hand to the small of her back. How could roping make her hurt everywhere?

Still, she had to clean Ace's hooves. She was going

to ask him to carry her on a long trip across the range. The least she could do was take care of his feet.

With her teeth set so hard that she heard a pop where her jaw hinged, Sam lowered herself close enough to the ground that she could pick up a hoof.

She'd only worked at the task a couple of seconds when she felt Jake's gaze on her, and looked up.

He gave her an admiring half smile and a pat on the shoulder.

"Keep after it, Brat. You just may end up a cowgirl, after all."

Chapter Thirteen ❧

The next morning came way too soon.

"Oh, wow," Sam sighed, sitting on the corner of her bed.

She shouldn't need a rest five minutes after waking up, but she'd had the coordination of a noodle-armed clown just trying to pull on her boots and jeans.

It will be worth it when we're out on the range, Sam promised herself, then walked downstairs to start her day.

"I don't know where he could be," Brynna was saying as Sam pushed open the door to the kitchen.

"It's the nice weather," Gram said. "We've had dogs take off before, this time of year."

"But Blaze?" Brynna said.

"Lots of times they come home with a snout full of porcupine quills," Gram said. "Those big porkies don't have much patience for being sniffed and pawed."

Brynna glanced up at Sam. "When was the last time you saw him?"

"I can't remember," she admitted.

She'd been so busy yesterday, she didn't recall seeing Blaze even once. Would she have noticed him, tagging along at her heels? Probably not, and that made her feel even worse.

"But Gram, last night—no, the night before, when you were sitting on the porch and Tempest was acting up—didn't you say Blaze was sleeping over by the bunkhouse?"

"You're right," Gram said. "That's the last time I saw him. Oh well, he'll come home when he's ready."

Sam wasn't so sure of that, and neither was Brynna.

"Before I leave for work, I think I'll give Leah a call and tell her he's missing," Brynna said, picking up the phone.

Leah Kenworthy was Jen's mom. Sam was pretty sure she knew what Brynna was thinking—their protective Border Collie could have left the ranch in search of Linc Slocum's hounds.

"Hi Leah, sorry to call so early," Brynna said. She chuckled, and Sam supposed Leah had said she'd been up for hours. "I'm almost ready to leave for work and just realized Blaze, our Border Collie, hasn't been around for about twenty-four hours."

Brynna listened. She nodded and a look of relief came over her face. "I can hear them baying. That must be driving you crazy. Yeah, I know. We all put up with a lot, just so we can earn our daily bread. Well, we'd really appreciate it if you let us know if you do. Thanks."

"They haven't seen him," Sam concluded as Brynna hung up.

"Right, and she told me the same thing you did, Grace," Brynna said to Gram. "She chalked up his wandering to spring fever. Still, it's good to know Linc's hounds are still in their kennel."

Sam noticed Brynna's eyes had come to rest on her, but she didn't ask what her stepmother was thinking. If it was anything that would delay tomorrow's campout, she didn't want to know.

Since no River Bend stock needed to be eartagged or branded, Dad had Sam practice on scrap leather.

"It's not the same," Dad said. He handed her a tool that looked like a cross between a stapler and a hole puncher. "But it's about the only way to practice."

Dad showed her how to load the tagger with River Bend's tags. They were light blue and carried the initials RBR for River Bend Ranch, and the ranch telephone number.

"Gold Dust uses purple tags," Dad explained, "and Three Ponies still does it the old-fashioned way. They use an under-seven."

"Under seven?" Sam asked.

Dad made a gesture next to his own ear. "Takin' a really sharp pocket knife, they cut the underside of the calf's ear. Two quick moves and there's a distinctive ear shape."

Sam shuddered. She closed her eyes and sucked in her suddenly queasy stomach.

Cowgirl. Rancher. Buckaroo. She wanted to be all three, but she had to admit the truth.

"Dad, I'll help Jen mark the Gold Dust calves with the purple ear tags, but Three Ponies is on its own. There's no way I'm going to"—Sam held her hand out as if it gripped a knife—"do that."

Dad nodded. "Good thing, too, 'cause Luke's downright picky when it comes to marking his stock."

"Why do we have to do things to their ears?" Sam asked. "They already have brands so that we know they're ours."

Dad studied her for a second, but Sam didn't get the feeling he thought she was being a wimp.

"If they're dirty, or covered with snow, or all bunched in together, it can be hard to read the brand," Dad explained. "Now practice on this leather, and make your moves quick."

Sam practiced. Each time she closed the tagger, she did it fast.

Although it probably wasn't exactly the same, a painful memory affected her technique.

She and Aunt Sue had been in a shopping mall near San Francisco when Sam had begged to get her ears pierced. Aunt Sue had given in, but the girl in the mall shop was a new employee. She'd looked more nervous than Sam had felt.

"You might want to wait," Aunt Sue had hinted, but Sam was afraid Aunt Sue would change her mind.

"Now or never," Sam had said stubbornly, and boy, had she been sorry.

The hesitant girl had made three attempts before she got the tiny gold stud through Sam's ear.

Now, Sam closed the tagger with a decisive snap. No way would she leave a little calf with a tender, aching ear like she'd had.

When it came time to practice branding, she at least knew how to do one thing right.

Building the branding fire was easy. She'd made campfires, and this was the same.

Dad lectured her some more while the branding iron, shaped in a backward *F* for Forster, heated in the fire.

"The design on the iron has to be simple. Don't want it blurred if the calf moves." Dad paused and shook his head. "Since you're learnin' this for real, guess there's no harm in telling you an example, sort of as a warning."

"I want to do it right," Sam said.

"Okay. Linc wanted a real complicated brand at first. He didn't like Jed's Diamond K, and thought he could put his whole name on his stock. That kinda detail calls for a real thin iron. Too thin. It sliced right through the calves' hides."

Dad's description created an awful image of bawling, disfigured animals.

"Why does he do things like that?" Sam demanded.

"Ignorance," Dad said. "He doesn't know any better."

"Dad . . ." Sam said. She hadn't meant to use an accusing tone, but Dad was being too kind in his assessment.

"Okay." Dad allowed the correction. "Linc Slocum doesn't understand that the ranch has to come first, before everything else. Even family."

Sam blinked in surprise. She sure hadn't expected Dad to say that.

"Family changes, but each generation depends on the ranch," Dad explained. "If we don't treat it right, we'll lose it."

Stiffly, Dad lifted the branding iron from the fire, blew on the ashy, backward *F*, then patiently returned it to heat some more.

"Linc won't ever understand," Sam insisted. "He doesn't depend on the ranch, or cattle, or even people! He counts on money to get himself out of trouble!"

As Sam's words exploded, she realized anger had been gnawing at her since Dad's fall.

Linc Slocum had been using those dogs for fun, but they could have killed Dad.

And Linc didn't care.

She wouldn't admit it to anyone, not Dad, Brynna, Gram, or even Jen, but she wanted something bad to happen to Linc Slocum, something that couldn't be solved with money.

There were always consequences for *her* thoughtless actions. When would Linc Slocum have to pay — and not in dollars — for his mistakes?

"Sometimes life ain't fair," Dad admitted. "Now, let me see you practice with this iron."

As quick as that, Dad had changed the subject.

Or maybe he hadn't seen it as a different subject. There was something in the way Dad handed her the heavy iron that said he expected her to fulfill her responsibilities to River Bend Ranch, fair or not.

"It's a waste of time and stress to handle a calf more than once," Dad was saying. "By the time you nod off tonight, you'll have learned how to vaccinate a calf, mark its ear, and slap on its brand, all in a few seconds. And it'll be done 'til next year. Okay?"

"Okay," Sam said.

She'd buckle down and work hard, but she still hoped Linc Slocum got what was coming to him.

*

Like gold ore veining a gray rock, dawn sent spindles of light across the early morning sky.

Sam and Jen had talked about using a packhorse to carry a tent, food, a roll of orange plastic fencing, the tagger, and branding irons, but they'd decided against it.

The ride out would be fine, but what about the trip back?

Herding a group of range-wild cattle that had been wily enough to escape the first roundup would be hard. Keeping them together would be even harder.

The rope leading back to another horse would only get in the way if they had to gallop after a fugitive.

So the girls packed only what was necessary.

Despite their heavily laden saddlebags and the burdens tied on behind the cantles, both horses felt their riders' excitement.

Ace snorted and broke into high-spirited bucking as they rode out of sight of the ranch.

"S-stop it," Sam scolded, after a teeth-cracking jump and a swerve that nearly unseated her.

Tossing her creamy mane, Silly neighed and shied away from Ace.

"Oh yes, I know you're terrified." Jen pretended to sympathize with her palomino.

Red Hereford cows and calves scattered at their approach for the first two hours of their ride.

The warm, windless morning allowed them to

make good time to the section of range that hadn't been searched for cattle.

As they started up the foothills between War Drum Flats and Arroyo Azul, the terrain changed from alkali flats and sagebrush to pinion pines and hardy grasses.

She heard the gurgle of a stream, but the area Sam thought she'd recognized wasn't quite familiar.

"I don't remember riding here before," Sam said.

"It's changed some," Jen said. "There was a lot of damage from that last storm. Water rushed through there." Jen nodded in the direction of a hillside that was still the color of chocolate milk. Swoops of earth had been shaped by powerful rains that had fallen the night Tempest was born.

"Look!" Sam pointed. "A lightning strike brought that tree down."

The black scar on the tree trunk was almost hidden by fallen branches from the grove around it. The storm had lashed the branches loose, or maybe the fallen tree had brought them down with it.

"Easy," Jen said when Silly lifted her golden knees and snorted.

Ace's nostrils worked loudly, then he turned, ears pointed back the way they'd come.

What did the horses sense? Sam met Jen's eyes. They both knew it was smart to pay attention to animals' warnings.

Silly fought her reins, eyes rolling. She took a few

steps that would have become a run if Jen hadn't turned her in a circle.

"It's just wind making those pine needles ripple," Jen said to comfort her horse.

"Jen, it's not windy," Sam said.

"I know that," Jen said under her breath. "Do you think I'm going to tell her there's something *alive* hiding under those fallen trees?"

Goose bumps raced down Sam's legs and chilled her, despite her leather chaps.

"I have a feeling she's about to find out anyway."

Chapter Fourteen ❦

The hounds surged up the hillside from behind them.

Sam looked in time to see the dogs' noses rise from the ground. Ears streaming back from their faces, the dogs ran silent and swift.

"Silly," Jen talked to her horse in a warning tone. "You know those dogs. Easy, girl."

Ace knew them too, but he didn't like them. With the dogs still half a mile away, Ace struck out with both hind feet as if he'd send them bowling back down the hillside if they came a step closer.

Pine needles rushed. Branches bobbed. Pointed hooves hit wood. All at once a huge buck, his many-pointed antlers held high, thrust up from the camouflage of the fallen tree.

Both horses shied, but the hounds cried as one, running faster, rejoicing at their success in flushing prey from his hiding place.

Golden legs striking the air, Silly slewed sideways, avoiding the dogs as Ace's head darted forward in threat.

The dogs ignored the horses.

In a single leap, the buck cleared the fallen branches, touched down, then moved like magic ahead of the dogs. Once, he stopped to look back at them. He aimed ears shaped like cupped palms toward the dogs, as if he'd never heard anything like their baying.

And, Sam guessed, he probably hadn't.

"Run, you stupid thing!" Jen yelled.

The buck did, gliding away with all three dogs after him.

"It's what they're trained for. It's not their fault," Sam muttered as she rubbed Ace's neck. "I'm trying to remember that," she told Jen. "I'm going to tell Brynna and she'll turn that fool in."

Sam looked back toward River Bend Ranch. If it wouldn't mean an end to their campout, she'd return to report Linc Slocum to Brynna now. Or maybe Sheriff Ballard. How cool would it be if he put Linc Slocum in jail?

"Jen, why would Linc turn them loose again?"

Silly answered instead. Her floating, friendly

neigh shattered the quiet that had settled as the dogs moved off.

Jen followed Sam's gaze, then twisted in her saddle to gaze in the same direction as Silly.

Jen sighed and pushed her glasses farther up her nose.

"Speak of the devil," she said. "I guess you can ask him yourself."

Golden Champagne, the biggest of the Kenworthy palominos, was nicknamed Champ. He was earning that name now, as he continued toward Sam and Jen, in spite of Linc Slocum, who sawed a severe, silver-mounted bit back and forth in Champ's mouth.

Sam's anger grew hotter. If the palomino followed his rider's directions, he'd be slogging through the downed branches the deer had just abandoned.

Instead, Champ used his horse sense to keep his rider safe, and paid for it with a sore mouth.

"What's all this carryin' on up here?" Linc bellowed.

Linc wore a brown shirt with gold piping, full-length, fancy chaps with his name branded on them, a long duster better suited for a Hollywood cowboy, and brass spurs with sharp rowels.

Sam's anger was about to boil over, when Jen noticed her.

"Down, girl," Jen whispered to Sam.

"I am so mad at him. My dad, the dogs, the way

he treats Champ . . ."

"You're hyperventilating," Jen said quietly. "That could make you pass out."

Sam's breaths came fast and loud, as if she were pulling in enough oxygen to tackle Slocum from the saddle. Oh, how she wanted to do it.

Slocum yanked his reins, jerking Champ to a stop. Then, Linc raised a silver whistle to his lips. His cheeks ballooned out and turned red as he blew.

Sam snugged her reins, staying in touch with Ace's mouth in case he bolted. She didn't hear the whistle, so she was pretty sure Slocum was blowing a high-pitched tone to summon the dogs. She didn't know if the horses could hear it.

Next, Slocum unhooked a bag hanging from the horn of his silver-mounted saddle. Swaying, he hefted the bag with both hands and upended it.

Chunks of meat tumbled out onto the ground.

"Sam?" Jen's voice penetrated Sam's anger. "If you pass out, I'm not carrying you home."

Sam guessed that meant she was still hyperventilating. She pressed her lips closed for a few seconds before she answered.

"I'm okay. I won't say . . . much," she promised.

Ace, for one, didn't believe her. Anger must have telegraphed down the reins, because the bay mustang sidestepped stiffly away from Champ as the palomino touched noses with Silly.

The whistle had worked. The dogs came bounding back.

With a satisfied smirk, Slocum slipped the whistle back in his pocket and turned to Sam and Jen.

"I suppose you girls are gonna tell on me," Slocum said, not sounding a bit embarrassed.

Sam searched her brain for something to say. Nothing she came up with was right.

She stared up the mountain, hoping for a glimpse of the white-tailed buck escaping.

When she turned back, Linc's face wore a gloating look as he watched the dogs swirl around Champ's legs. They gulped the meat until only one fist-sized hunk was left, then the black-and-tan one, Shirley, turned on the others with a snarl. They jumped back, tails wagging low, and let her choke it down.

Slocum patted the rifle in his saddle sheath.

"I could've let them run him to a standstill," he bragged. "Or gotten 'em to chase him back into that box canyon he came outta." He jerked his thumb toward a shady defile below.

"I'm glad you didn't," Jen said quickly.

Slocum didn't seem to notice her level, lifeless tone as he went on.

"I would've sent Ryan out with you two," Slocum continued. "But he's obsessed with that mongrel foal. He's actin' like a danged nursemaid."

Sam didn't remind Slocum that he'd promised

the foal to her when he'd discovered his expensive Appaloosa mare was in foal to an outlaw stallion named Diablo.

She didn't mention the mongrels' sire was a valuable endurance champion, either.

Sam only said, "Foals can take a lot of time and attention, especially when they have first-time mothers."

Too bad her polite efforts were wasted on Slocum.

He actually gave a snort before saying, "There's something unmanly about the way he hovers over it."

"No," both girls protested.

Sam noticed Jen's voice had an even sharper edge than hers.

When Sam glanced over, she saw Jen was gripping the saddle horn so hard, her knuckles had turned white.

Jen and Ryan weren't exactly boyfriend and girlfriend, but almost. Still, Jen found the control not to interrupt Linc's ranting.

"I'm having Hotspot bred back before long," he said, "sending her over to Sterling's stable, to their Appaloosa stallion Cloud Cap.

"My son says the mare's too *nervous*," Slocum's voice took on a mocking, high-pitched tone. Then he actually spat into the dirt and all three dogs looked up in surprise. "That stud's the only horse around with bloodlines to match hers and I'm done listening to my boy's whining."

Sam had never liked Ryan more than she did in that moment.

She'd bet Ryan was right. He'd been exercising, watching, and coddling Hotspot since he'd arrived from England. He'd know if it was too soon for the mare to be bred again.

She crossed her fingers, hoping Ryan won this battle with his father.

"Mr. Slocum, are you taking the dogs home now?" Sam asked. "Range cattle are kind of spooky to begin with, so they're difficult to herd."

"Yeah," Slocum said. "So, what's your point?"

Jen tried to force a smile, but it faltered. Sam could almost see her switch to using her brain instead of her manners.

Jen pushed her glasses up her nose before she explained, "The range cattle, being feral, might hide if they hear the dogs."

"Gotcha," Slocum said. "I plan on takin' them away. It's my plan, though, and it's got nothing to do with you or your cows, Forster."

Sam met Linc's eyes. He didn't match her attempts to be polite, so why should she even try?

"Got 'em under control," he boasted, looking down at the dogs. "They're loyal to me now."

When Slocum patted his saddlebags, Sam almost laughed. He must have more meat, and wasn't that typical? Instead of learning to work with the dogs and earning their love and loyalty, he'd found a way to buy them off.

I don't care, as long as he leaves, Sam thought, and minutes later, he did.

"Jen . . ." Sam began.

"Can we not talk about him right now?" Jen said. "I'm nauseous from keeping in what I really think of that—"

"Later," Sam agreed. "There's no way in the world I'm going to let him ruin this fantastic day on the range."

Jen still couldn't manage a smile, but she gave Sam a hearty thumbs-up, and together they rode up the mountain in peace.

It didn't take long for the broad blue sky and calling birds to bring the girls back to the task at hand.

"According to my dad, there are only two dangerous places where cattle might hide in this section," Jen said.

"Cow Killer Caldera?" Sam said, because Dallas had mentioned it to her.

"That's one," Jen said, nodding, "although I have to tell you, I'm not convinced it's really a caldera. Do those mountains look volcanic to you?"

Sam considered the sand-colored peaks, then admitted, "Unless I saw lava and smoke boiling out of them, I don't think I'd know, Jen."

"Most people wouldn't," Jen said generously. "But a caldera is formed when the center of a volcano collapses in, and it's supposed to be way deep." She shrugged. "I guess we'll see when we get up there."

"What's the other dangerous place?" Sam asked.

"There's a thorn thicket about level with that plateau, and it doesn't even have a name, as far as I know."

As they rode on, Sam couldn't help appreciating how smart Jen was.

"You know that spiny thicket, though?" Jen mused. "I bet it's just brush. Thorns don't exactly flourish in northern Nevada. Sam, are you yawning?"

"No," Sam assured her, although the confrontation with Slocum had worn her out. "At least, not because you're boring. Dad's been working me hard these last couple of days. It's like he said 'yes,' then made me pay for it."

"My dad, too," Jen said, then her smile was back and Sam's spirits perked up as Jen's grin turned impish. "But our dads aren't here now."

"No," Sam said, "and do you know what I have in my saddlebags?"

Jen let her head fall back on her neck in anticipation. "Something wonderful cooked by your grandmother?"

"Chocolate chip cookies *and* brownies!"

"Oh my gosh." Jen sighed. "And my mom made a

caramel pecan cake and gave me *half.*"

"When we stop for lunch —" Sam began, and then she drew rein.

Jen slowed Silly and looked back, brows raised, over her shoulder.

"We don't have to wait for lunch," Sam said. "If we want to eat dessert at" — she glanced at her watch — "ten thirty-two, we can."

"Yeah," Jen said, but her sensible side made one last demand. "How about if we just ride up to the plateau? Then we'll be halfway to the top."

"Sounds good to me, partner," Sam said, then she touched her heels to Ace and rode smiling into the morning.

"You have chocolate all over your cheeks," Jen said, later.

"Have you checked your eyelashes lately?" Sam asked.

With the horses ground-tied nearby, the friends leaned back on their elbows and closed their eyes. Through sun-struck eyelids, Sam wondered when they'd see the wild horses.

In spite of the changes made by winter snows and spring rain, she'd recognized the area. They weren't far from the Arroyo Azul shortcut to the Phantom's hidden valley.

Standing down below, the steep shelf overlooking

the plateau was invisible. But the shelf was narrow, barely wide enough for a single horse, so they'd remained on the plateau for their picnic.

It was probably a bad idea to let Ace and Silly wander, Sam thought, as the horses moved off a few steps. But both horses obeyed ground-tying, and she was feeling too full and drowsy to go after them.

Then she heard the snort. It hadn't come from Silly or Ace.

"Jen," she whispered.

Jen opened her eyes, already alert.

Sam turned her head slowly toward the sound.

New Moon stood at the other side of the plateau.

If a black jewel existed, something like a diamond but dark as night, that's what Moon's coat resembled.

When she'd seen the young stallion by moonlight at River Bend, she'd known he was beautiful. Now, his shining, satiny coat made him magnificent.

Did he recognize her? The delicate trembling of his ear tips made Sam imagine he did, until Jen brought her back to reality.

"Our horses," Jen hissed.

Of course, Sam thought. Why else would Moon venture so near to humans? He was recruiting for his tiny herd.

Behind him, a red bay swished her tail. A bald-faced mare with blue eyes and a black foal stamped a hoof.

Moon nickered an offer that brought both domestic horses' heads up.

Silly's nostrils vibrated. Her head tilted to one side so that her forelock fell away from her brown eyes. Fascinated by the mustangs, the palomino broke into a trot. Reins trailing, she went to investigate the wild ones.

Chapter Fifteen ∽

Oh no. Sam didn't gasp aloud.

Trying not to spook Ace and Silly, she joined Jen in a scrabble across the bare rock.

"Oof!" Both girls knocked the wind from themselves as they tackled the trailing reins before either horse got very far.

Moon's head rose, showing the long line of his midnight throat. He neighed his disappointment and Silly whinnied back.

"No you don't," Jen snapped, as she stood up.

Then, for better control, Jen gripped the reins just beneath the palomino's chin.

All the wild horses startled at Jen's sudden height.

The bald-faced mare nipped the bay, herding her.

So, you're the lead mare, Sam thought. With the delicate black foal tucked against her side and Moon at her heels, the bald-faced bay took her few followers away.

"That could have been bad," Jen sighed.

"Losing our horses on the morning of our first day?" Sam joked. "Naw, I'm sure our dads would understand."

They laughed, promised each other they wouldn't make that mistake again, then got serious about searching for cattle.

As they rode, staring in opposite directions so that they missed nothing, Sam thought about the black foal. It had been older than Tempest, with a blockier head and bigger bones.

Moon couldn't have fathered it, because he'd had no herd of his own last year. And she didn't remember seeing the bald-faced, blue-eyed mare in the Phantom's band.

For a minute, Sam concentrated on whose mare Moon had stolen, but then she smiled. There was a more important, more exciting aspect to the wild black colt.

He wasn't Moon's, but Moon had obviously adopted him.

"Yeah!" Sam muttered under her breath.

"See one?" Jen asked. The lenses of her glasses looked cloudy with dust as she peered past Sam.

Then, before Sam could explain Brynna's awful

lecture on murderous stallions, Sam saw the cattle.

Just yards away, two big white faces rose above a stand of sagebrush. Jaws suddenly still, the Herefords quit chewing and stared. Just below the cows' chins, two tiny white faces did the same.

Oh my gosh! Sam thought, but she mouthed the words, "Right there."

Afraid the wild cattle would stampede, Sam didn't raise her arm to point. She hardly breathed.

They were River Bend cows. Somehow, Sam recognized them from a winter hay drop, even before the cows' ears, tagged in blue, flickered her way.

Their pink-rimmed eyes looked bloodshot. Brush and stickers had snagged in their coats, but they were River Bend cows, and their calves were worth at least a thousand dollars apiece.

Now what? Sam knew she and Jen had decided to gather all the cattle they could, pen them with the plastic fencing, then brand them tomorrow afternoon.

But the reality of these cautious cattle made her wonder if that was possible.

The cattle she'd driven before had already been milling in a herd. Now, staring into eyes that were not only wild, but fierce, Sam wasn't sure how the "gather" part would work.

"Hey there, bossy," Jen crooned to the cows.

Sam stared at her friend. Jen's voice was as melodic as birdsong.

A quick bawling moo came from one cow. The others shuffled in place, but Jen kept talking. The cattle seemed fascinated and finally Sam realized Jen wasn't just babbling bovine flattery.

The cows must remember the winter hay drops that had kept them nourished when snow covered the sparse grass. To them, human voices meant food.

"Hey, Sam, remember that box canyon Linc mentioned? Oh, yes, you sweet-smelling, bug-eyed beauty, I see that brindle baby. Wow, mama cow, how did you ever come up with that Halloween peanut-butter swirl coat and that pure white face for your baby? Well, I'm thinking, Sam, I'm talking to you now. Sammy, pal, stay with me."

"Mm-hm?" Sam hummed, trying not to distract the hypnotized Herefords.

"If we can ease this bunch back down to the box canyon, we can put the plastic fencing across the mouth of it. Then we'll have a perfect place to hold them and brand them—Oh no, mama cow, I didn't say brand. No, no, no. Easy. Okay, you want to start back that way? What a good idea."

Jen's eyebrows lifted above her glasses as the cows shuffled out of the sagebrush and headed downhill.

Ace trembled with excitement, eager to chase after the cattle, but Sam held him in.

Jen let the cattle get well ahead, so they wouldn't feel pressured. Silly must have forgotten the mustangs, because she followed calmly at an uncharacteristic, flat-footed walk.

The trail was more than a deer path. It was about two horse widths wide and flanked with sagebrush.

Jen moved to the right of the trail, so Sam aimed Ace toward the left.

The cow with the brindle calf looked back over her shoulder with a cautious moo. When she took a few steps left, Ace mirrored her movements. Even though they were half a football field behind, the cows and calves returned to the center of the road.

"Good work," Sam whispered, but she'd known this would happen. She wasn't the cattle expert; Ace was.

Hazing the cattle into the box canyon was easy. Three of the four animals trotted in as if they'd been headed this way all day, but the brindle calf looked up, startled, as if the canyon walls were closing in on her.

With a cry, she sprinted past Jen.

"Hold 'em." Jen snapped. Silly pivoted and set off after the calf.

Three anxious faces, one bawling to the brindle calf, looked after the runaway.

Lowering himself into his cutting horse stance, Ace advanced on the cattle and they backed away.

Ears flattened and head lowered, Ace held the cattle until the brindle calf galloped past. Headed for her mom, the calf kicked her heels, lashed her tail in a corkscrew, then straightened it, as if it propelled her dash.

Sam and Jen didn't take time for celebration. They unrolled the plastic fence and erected it across the mouth of the box canyon.

"Okay!" Jen cheered once the cattle had raced for the far end of the canyon, away from the commotion of fencing. "Time to find some Gold Dust cows."

"I guess we'll have to take turns," Sam said as they both took long drinks from their canteens.

"Yeah, they'd probably be okay if we left them," Jen said slowly. "But if those hounds returned, they'd run right through that fencing."

"So, one of us stays with the herd here, while the other goes out brush-poppin'?"

Jen nodded. "But we both have to promise, absolutely, to go where we say we will. Like if I tell you I'll ride to the top of that ridge and stay between that big black rock and that deformed-looking pinion pine? I'll stay there."

"Okay," Sam agreed.

"That way, if Silly comes running down without me because she saw a rabid butterfly or something, you'll know where to come looking."

"What about my herd?" Sam asked. "You know, my dad says the ranch comes first and those cows—"

"Sam!" Jen stretched the word out in surprise. "I'm more important than—yeah, very funny," she said as Sam began laughing.

Jen swung Silly's head to face the trail. "Just for that, I go first and you have guard duty. *Adios*," she called over her shoulder, and then she was gone.

The day seemed to get hotter every minute that Jen was gone.

Sam stared up the hill. She knew where Jen had gone, but they hadn't agreed upon how long she'd be there.

Sam took a packet of jerky from her saddlebag and munched on it as a horseback lunch. After all that cake, she really didn't want much else.

After nursing their calves, the River Bend cattle had folded their legs and lay dozing. Sam relaxed with them, hoping Slocum had gotten his hounds safely home. If dogs were trained to chase a buck as big as the one they'd seen, they'd have no qualms about tackling Moon's little black colt. To herself, Sam had already named the colt Night.

Ace snorted and looked up the hill. Sam followed his glance. Two cows with purple ear tags trotted down the trail. One had a calf.

That made three, Sam thought. There were three calves to vaccinate, earmark, and brand.

Sam's hand closed as if she were squeezing the earmarking gun. *Not 'til tomorrow*, she told herself. That was soon enough.

The cows Jen was herding stopped when they saw Sam. She backed Ace. Step by grudging step, he moved away from the entrance to the box canyon, but he didn't like it.

Head lowered, Ace kept an eye on the cattle inside, even though they gave no sign of rising to their feet when Sam jumped down and opened the plastic fence.

"Amazing," Jen sighed once the fence was fastened back in place. "How's that for a Father's Day present?"

"Better than a card and a box of peanut brittle!" Sam crowed.

Until dusk turned the range purple-gray, the girls took turns riding out and searching. Their good luck had peaked early, though, because they found no more strays.

The two River Bend cows, two Gold Dust cows, and three calves milled uneasily in their box canyon corral while Sam and Jen built a campfire for warmth.

"They're sure noisy," Sam said as the cattle bawled at each other.

"Dad told me when they haven't run together, cattle aren't always friendly to each other," Jen said.

The girls ate bread, cheese, and salami, not bothering to assemble sandwiches, as they watched the two Brangus stare and moo at the River Bend Herefords.

"I hope they stop grouching at each other before

we bed down for the night," Jen said.

"I bet they'll be friends by tomorrow," Sam said. "I hope we can find some more."

"It's Slocum's section," Jen reminded her. "You might not find any more from River Bend."

"I know," Sam said as she unrolled her sleeping bag. "I'll be satisfied with what we've got."

"But not happy?" Jen asked, untying the knots on her bedroll.

A cricket's chirp interrupted their conversation and Sam smiled. "I'm happy already, just because we got to do this."

"Me too," Jen said.

Once they'd wiggled into their sleeping bags, the cows limited their complaints to loud snuffles. The fire crackled from inside the circle of rocks they'd built to contain it.

Staring into the star-studded darkness overhead, Sam decided to ride back to the plateau tomorrow. She wanted to see Moon again, but more than that, she hoped to see the Phantom.

With luck, the two stallions would keep their bands apart, but she'd still get to see them.

The stars were blurring in her sleepy gaze when Sam gradually became aware of howling.

"They don't sound like coyotes," Sam said.

She raised up on one elbow and looked at Jen.

Jen's face looked strangely bare without her glasses.

"They're not," Jen said, sounding wide awake.

"Could we hear those hounds from here if they were at the Gold Dust?"

"I don't know," Jen said. "Sound travels in weird ways."

The hounds stopped howling. For a minute, Sam heard only the hobbled horses, pawing and chewing grass.

Sam lay back down. She stared at the sky again, not turning to face Jen as she asked, "How do you stand him? Living there on that ranch and seeing him every day. . . . You're a stronger, nicer person than I am. I'd go crazy."

She didn't tell Jen her ugly hope, that somehow Linc Slocum would fall into a situation he couldn't buy his way out of.

"I think of how I felt when I thought we were moving back into town," Jen said.

Sam shivered and wiggled farther down into her sleeping bag until her toes touched the bottom. She took a deep breath of high desert air perfumed with sagebrush and pine.

A city campout would be scented with car exhaust and the contents of the nearest Dumpster.

"That'd work for me, too," Sam said.

When Jen said nothing else, she thought her best friend had fallen asleep.

Sam was drowsing, too, when Jen whispered, "Sam?"

"What?" She jumped.

"I didn't mean to scare you, but do you want any dessert?"

"We didn't have much dinner," Sam said, yawning. "But no, I think that the cake and the salami pretty much filled me up."

"Yeah, me too," Jen said. "But those chocolate chip cookies have walnuts, right? And nuts have lots of protein."

"I see what you're saying." Sam giggled. "They're good for us. We really should have just one before we fall asleep."

Chapter Sixteen ∾

Clouds lay like snow on the plateau as Sam rode up the cattle path the next morning.

Sam looked back over her shoulder to see Jen's legs braced far apart as she stood with her cup of cocoa in the mouth of the box canyon. She waved as Sam rode away.

They'd camped out alone and held a herd of cattle all night long.

Okay, so it was a small herd, but the cattle hadn't pushed down the fence to escape overnight, and that was an accomplishment. Sam felt proud.

Above her, the clouds were drifting from the plateau.

Good, she thought. Clear weather would make it

easier to spot what she was looking for—not just cattle, but mustangs.

Sam pushed up the sleeves of her green sweatshirt. The morning was warm and Ace frisked like a yearling. Sam felt so good, she let him swing into a lope.

Wind stirred by his gait snatched Sam's Stetson from her head. Held on by its stampede string, her hat bounced against her back as she swayed in the saddle, forgetting Slocum and his dogs, absorbing the green-and-gold scenery as it slipped past.

Dew revived the wet clay smell of the plateau. Sun awakened the tang of sagebrush. Sam drew the scents of home into her lungs, smiling until Ace sensed the mustangs.

His sudden, jolting trot sent shocks through Sam's spine, which was sensitive from sleeping on the ground.

Ace clambered up the incline, then stopped without warning on the plateau.

Sam's elbows drew close to her body. In fact, every muscle and tendon hugged closer to her bones as she tried to make herself smaller.

She felt as if she'd stepped onto a stage while a play was in progress.

Moon and his mares stood off to her right. The Phantom's band grazed and milled to her left. The Phantom's big honey-brown lead mare flattened her ears at a bay horse within her band. The bay looked familiar even before he turned to show Sam the patch of white over one eye.

Pirate! Sam smiled, remembering the colt she'd first seen on Dad and Brynna's wedding day. He'd come through the winter strong and tall.

Ace snorted, arched his neck, and pawed. Sam's fingers curved around the reins, pulling them snug. She wouldn't blame the little gelding if he bolted. He'd been wild, and the temptation to run toward one of the herds might be too much.

But then Sam understood Ace wasn't agitated by the mustangs; he just recognized a friend.

"It's him," Sam whispered.

The silver stallion moved through his band until he stood in front of his mares. He was the most beautiful horse in the world. And for one instant, he saw and greeted her.

Prancing forward, the Phantom tossed his head. Muscles sculpted the brightness of his neck. His mane and forelock rayed around him. Touched by the rising sun, he was a magical beast wreathed in a sunburst.

My Zanzibar, Sam thought. In all the world the stallion recognized just one human as a friend, and it was her.

His single whinny was for her, but then he turned his eyes on New Moon.

Moon's neigh rung out, only to be covered by the Phantom's. In the silence that followed, the stallions faced each other, ears tilted forward. Then each snorted. Each struck out a front hoof at the same moment.

Sam held her breath as, together, the stallions squealed loudly and rose into half rears.

Last fall, the Phantom had tried scolding his son with the snaking gesture he used to herd mares and foals.

Last fall, Moon had hesitated, lowered his head, and lost.

Since then, Moon had grown up.

When the silver stallion bobbed his head, higher with each movement, the black stallion did the same.

Moon was taller than his father, Sam realized.

The young stallion arched his tail and flexed his neck as if he knew his black head was inches closer to the sky.

Sam's fingers froze to her reins. She couldn't turn Ace away from the fight and go looking for cattle. She had to see this battle through.

Moon was more muscular, stronger than the last time he'd challenged his sire, and though Brynna insisted fights between stallions were mostly play-acting, these two looked serious.

The Phantom trumpeted an arrogant neigh that gave Sam chills.

Look at me, king of kings, mightiest of mustangs!

The silver stallion trembled with his own power. He wasn't bluffing. He'd just given his son a chance to walk away, unbeaten.

Moon didn't take the Phantom's offer.

Black knees silvered by sunshine, he trotted forward until he reached the Phantom. Moon snorted so loudly, a red roan mare with white sprinkling her back sprinted past the Phantom's lead mare to watch.

Moon was so close now, the stallions sniffed each other's ears, smelled each other's nostrils and breath.

This could end happily, Sam told herself. It could be a reunion, not a fight. But Moon hadn't forgotten he'd once, however briefly, ruled the Phantom's herd.

The black rose on his hind legs, but came down at once. With a forceful snap, his chin pounded the Phantom's withers.

Sam curled forward in the saddle. She gripped her reins with one hand while the other braced across her stomach. This would not end well.

Moon was exerting dominance he didn't have.

Surprised but unhurt, the Phantom stepped back, standing eye to eye with Moon. Sweat showed white on the young stallion's black coat as the Phantom pressed his forehead to Moon's.

When Moon didn't back down, the Phantom swerved as if to bite his son's glorious tail.

Moon mirrored the gesture and the stallions circled, head to tail, for what must have been a full minute. At last, Moon bit the Phantom's right heel, drawing first blood.

A scream of outrage erupted from the silver stallion.

He reared like a monster, mouth agape, tidal wave of mane cresting against the sky.

Moon was brave—no, *foolhardy*, Sam thought—ducking threshing hooves, going in low, trying to bite and grab and pull his sire off balance—but he failed.

The Phantom crashed down on Moon's back.

Did the plateau quake as the black stallion fell to his knees? It felt like it, and Sam ached for Moon. He was trapped there, until the Phantom struggled loose and backed off a step.

Silent and determined, Moon staggered to his feet.

The Phantom was taking no chances of a second assault. When Moon curved his neck and tucked in his chin, protecting his jugular vein, the Phantom bumped his shoulder, making the young stallion stumble. When Moon lunged with a wide-open mouth, the Phantom wheeled and released a kick into his son's hind legs. Each time Moon moved, the Phantom kept him off balance, reminding him he was not the ruler here.

Then both stallions grew alert. Arched necks flew up to their full length. Flattened ears pricked to listen. Snorting nostrils distended, drawing in the scent of trouble.

At first Sam didn't understand. Unconcerned, the mares grazed, nursed their foals, and stood head to tail, swishing cool air on each other's faces. Only the honey-colored mare seemed distracted.

Pirate and the roan filly had ambled away from their herd.

Night, Moon's adopted colt, had done the same. Noses touching, the three young horses made a truce.

The stallions didn't notice the disobedience within their bands. Front hooves stepping with spirit, panting from their battle, the black and silver stallions shifted to face the cattle trail.

Brush shook. Dirt scattered. Something was coming up the path to the plateau.

Was something wrong? Sam wondered. Could Jen be coming after her?

This time, the dogs didn't burst baying from the sagebrush. Their tails were straight up, wagging with excitement as they sized up the horses.

The herds stood, trembling with curiosity as the predators crouched lower, bellies almost touching the ground as they considered the strange, deer-like prey.

Should she yell at the dogs, or would that startle the herds, start them running, and begin the chase?

A dun mare gave a nervous nicker and backed with stuttering hooves into the safety of the Phantom's herd. Another mare called to her foal, then bolted forward, batting it with a swing of her head when it didn't move fast enough. The bald-faced mare neighed to Night.

Startled, maybe afraid he'd been caught playing with the young horses from the Phantom's herd,

Night bolted. He ran away from both bands and headed across the plateau alone.

Fleeing, he might have been a fawn.

His flight worked like a match to gasoline, setting the hounds into an explosion of barks, and then baying as they ran after him.

Chapter Seventeen ⚬

The stallions dropped their heads, herding Moon's mares, pushing them in with the larger band.

Sam couldn't believe her eyes. The enemies knew safety lay with the herd. They circled the joined band, nipping and neighing, trying to keep them together.

Ace snorted and his heels lashed out, though the dogs were far away. Sam kept him reined in and suddenly she was glad, because the bald-faced mare and Pirate bolted after the foal. If she'd allowed it, Ace would have been right with them.

Moon refused to let his mare go. He dealt her a harsh bite on the neck and she shied, but Pirate kept running. His hooves thundered across the plateau, after the dogs.

The pack was baying with such excitement, they couldn't have heard Pirate coming. But the brown pointer must have sensed him. The dog slowed and turned in an arc toward Pirate, and suddenly the pack shifted their attack. They chased the closer prey.

"No!" Sam screamed at the dogs. "Stop it!"

The black-and-tan hound leaped for Pirate's hind legs. As if time braked into slow motion, Sam saw a ribbon of bay skin peel back. Then she saw blood.

Pirate abandoned the rescue and returned to his herd. Faced by so many milling horses, the dogs hesitated, then looked back at Night.

The black foal shivered. His head drooped and his legs trembled.

The hound named Gator jumped into the air, mouth open as he aimed at a mare's nose.

He never made the bite.

The Phantom's heels caught the dog and sent him spinning away. Beside the white stallion, Moon moved into the same defensive positive, guarding the herd.

But what about Night?

Sam knew the answer even before the question finished flashing through her mind. The stallions had to protect the herd.

Hands shaking, Sam unsnapped her rope holder. She could only think of one way to make the colt an unappealing target.

"Here comes your chance to discipline those dogs," she told Ace.

If the dogs turned on Ace, she'd send him galloping for the safety of the herd and the protection of the stallions. That was an advantage Dad hadn't had when the dogs attacked Jeep.

The Phantom's head whipped in her direction, white mane flying as he watched her.

"Got me covered?" she mumbled to the stallion, but she knew better.

He was no longer her pet horse Blackie. If it came to a choice, the stallion must guard his herd. Not her.

Sam touched her heels to Ace and trotted toward Night.

"Easy, easy, easy," Sam told Ace when the dogs followed. "We're pretending we're in charge here."

With the dogs just a few yards from Ace's heels, Sam stopped short of Night and pulled her mustang around to face the pack.

Hope surged up in her when she saw the dogs were still making up their minds, still deciding whether she was some interfering creature or a master.

Whirling her rope over her head, she shouted, "Get back! Shirley, Bub, Gator, get back, I said!"

When the black-and-tan hound growled, chills rained down Sam's arms. It was a test, and Ace wanted to solve it with his heels. He squealed in frustration when she refused to let him whirl and kick. Thinking of Pirate's wound, she couldn't let him do it.

Instead, Sam used the rope like a whip.

Claws scrabbling, the dogs jumped back to avoid punishment.

"Bad dogs," she yelled. "Go home!"

Confused, the dogs pressed together for an instant.

Was it the safest time to drive Night to the herd? Or the most dangerous?

Sam swung Ace behind the foal, and suddenly they both knew what to do. They bolted toward the herd and Ace didn't stop until they were surrounded by others of their kind.

Slammed between a chestnut mare and the roan filly, Sam felt warm horseflesh press her legs. The blue-eyed mare crashed into them as she made for her colt. The noisy dun snapped at Ace and he squealed before giving her a frustrated nip.

Just the same, the nervous mass of horses meant safety while the hounds were near.

Suddenly the Phantom broke from the herd. Head low, ears flat, and mouth open, he moved like a striking snake after the dogs. Behind him, the honey-colored mare urged the combined herd across the plateau in the opposite direction.

Yapping, the speckled hound stood her ground for a minute, until Moon joined his father's charge.

Struggling with her rope and reins, doing her best to keep Ace from being swept along with the stampeding herd, Sam saw the dogs flee from the stallions.

Only Shirley paused in the cow trail and gave a single bark. Then, wagging her tail as if it had all been a game, she followed the others.

More than anything, Sam wanted to jump from Ace and run to the Phantom. Sweat had darkened his bright coat to pewter. He quivered with anger as he stared after the dogs.

Going to him wouldn't be safe, but Sam wanted to throw her arms around his mighty neck and hug him for his bravery.

And, she thought as she looked at Moon, his mercy.

She didn't do it.

When the Phantom wheeled away from the trail and the lingering scent of dogs, he raced past her. She thought his dark eyes met hers through his tangled forelock. For sure, his pale shoulder grazed her leg, as he stayed several galloping steps ahead of Moon.

And then all the mustangs were gone.

Sam was still shaking with reaction, still wondering how she could get her words in order to tell Jen what she'd seen, when the three Brangus cows—two adults with a calf in between—appeared on the trail ahead.

Ace halted. Sam swallowed hard.

They were huge and almost burgundy in color. Sam knew they were a common cross between Angus cattle and Brahmas. She knew they were valued for their quiet temperaments and that Jed Kenworthy, who'd probably put those purple tags in their ears, thought they were the best beef cattle on the range. But they blocked the trail, looking to Sam like maroon refrigerators with horns.

Ace wasn't intimidated. He jogged toward the cattle with casual authority.

Sam knew Ace was the expert and she was just along for the ride when the two cows glanced at each other, flapped their ears in agreement, then turned down the trail. Without a backward glance, all three trotted in front of Ace as if they'd been going that direction in the first place.

She'd only been gone two hours.

Sam couldn't believe it was only eight A.M. when she stood drinking water with her granola bar while Jen and Silly watched over the loud, cranky cattle penned in the box canyon.

Up on the plateau, fear or adrenaline had swept away her fury at Linc Slocum. Now she just wanted him punished.

"I hate it," Jen said, when Sam had finished telling her everything. "But I don't think we can do anything right now. Do you see any point in going back early? I mean, don't you think we should finish up here?"

"Yeah," Sam said. "But as soon as we get home, someone has to make him send those dogs back to Louisiana where it's legal for them to do what they do best. *Then*, he needs to be punished."

As they finished off their granola bars, they stared at the restless cattle.

"They know something's up," Jen said.

"I think you're right," Sam agreed, and now that her hands had stopped shaking, she knew there was no way to put off the only part of the trip she'd dreaded.

Sam swallowed hard and tried to assess her feelings. She still wasn't looking forward to hurting the calves, but it really was for their own good. She had to remember that. Besides, her hesitation would only cause them more pain.

Handling six fractious adult cattle while she and Jen vaccinated, branded, and ear-tagged four calves could be tricky.

"What are we waiting for?" Sam asked at last.

"It seems awfully early to start," Jen said, "but what if we run out of daylight?"

"We can't risk it," Sam agreed. "If we're late meeting them at War Drum Flats tomorrow morning, my dad will jump to the conclusion I've been trampled. Or thrown. Or carried away by a giant vulture."

So, even though they had the high-altitude Cow Killer Caldera left to check, they decided to get busy.

"If we finish early and find more cattle near the caldera, we'll just drive them along with the others," Jen said. "There's no reason the calves can't be branded later."

Unless they escape, Sam thought, but she didn't say

it. Instead she gave Ace the praise he deserved.

"How are you doing, best cow horse in the world?" Sam asked as she picked up Ace's trailing reins and kissed his nose.

He nudged Sam and stamped as if he was ready to go again. Sam swung into the saddle.

While Jen held it open, Sam rode through the small gap in the orange plastic fence. Then, from the saddle, she did the same for Jen.

Even before Sam could refasten the gate, Ace's eyes were on the cows and he was ready to work.

Sam wished the people who thought mustangs were scrubby and weak could test their papered purebreds against Ace. He'd already had a demanding morning, and now he was going to make her look like a real roper.

"I'll do it just like I did at home," Sam whispered to Ace. "I promise."

Sam's mind conjured a picture of Jake, rope wheeling gracefully above his head, and she did the same.

"Pretty," Jen complimented Sam's spinning loop, then she trotted Silly toward the first cow and calf. "This is going to be okay."

And it was.

As the first Brangus bolted away from Jen, her calf lagged behind. In a single leap, Ace positioned Sam to throw her rope for the calf's back hooves.

"In a minute," she told the horse, and they chased

him around once more so that she wouldn't have to drag him so far to the campfire.

The little purplish heels were moving back and kicking up. Sam focused. *Almost.* She concentrated. *Almost there.* She readied her loop, then launched her rope with the underhand flick Jake had taught her.

There!

"I got him!" she cried incredulously as Jen vaulted from the saddle to run to the calf. "First try!"

Jen gave a single nod before throwing herself on the wide-eyed calf.

Babbling sweet talk, Jen used her body to subdue the terrified, bucking creature. She pulled off the top of the hypodermic with her teeth, and dispensed the shot.

"Get down here!" she yelled.

Oh, yeah. Sam scrambled off Ace and held the calf while Jen applied the Gold Dust brand.

Coughing against the stench and sizzle of burning hair, Sam rushed to snap a tag through the calf's ear.

"We did it!" Sam yelled as they released the calf back to its mother. Jen was equally excited, but Ace backed away, shaking his head.

"Okay, I'll take it easy from here on out," Sam promised.

After that, roping the calves' heels was the easy part.

Noise was the hard part. For the first time, Sam understood why some sounds were called "deafening."

The mooing of cows and bawling calves crowded the air until she heard nothing else.

Jen kept working as the "calf mugger," just as Jake had hoped. Ace and Silly took turns as roping horse, and both understood when it was time to start backing toward the fire to get the hot branding iron.

The smell of burning hair clogged Sam's nostrils, just as the cacophony of cattle filled her ears.

All three Gold Dust calves and one River Bend calf had been reunited with their mothers, when Sam and Jen took a break.

From one corner of the box canyon, they watched the cows give licking comfort to their babies while fixing the girls with accusing glares.

"It's for his own good," Jen called to a Brangus mother whose moos had changed to incessant hoots.

"She doesn't believe you," Sam said, though Jen had echoed her own thoughts.

Jen leaned against a smooth rock in the canyon wall. She polished her glasses on her shirt hem, peered through them, then slipped them on.

"Your turn with the branding iron," Jen said.

A sigh gusted out before Sam could stop it.

"I know," she said.

I can do this, she thought as she swung back into the saddle. *I can.*

Sam roped the brindle calf easily. Jen vaccinated it, and the blue ear tag was clicked on before the mother cow went berserk.

Sam felt hypnotized as she squatted with the heavy branding iron. She focused on one square inch of red-brown hide. She'd put it right there. She raised the iron and had it poised over the calf's left hip, when Jen yelped.

Jen waved her arms as the mother cow lunged at her. Jen didn't want to run, but she didn't want to be butted, either.

"Do it!" Jen cried with one hand on the cow's head. "Hurry, so we can let her calf go."

Sam steadied her hand, trying to concentrate past the mayhem swirling around her.

She had lowered the smoking iron within an inch of the struggling calf when Jen shouted something else.

"What?" Sam shouted back in exasperation.

"Upside down!"

Is that what Jen had said?

"Up—?"

Oh my gosh. Sam fumbled to rotate the iron. She'd almost branded the brindle calf—already a standout in any herd—with the backward *F*, upside down.

Quickly, evenly, she pressed the iron down, then set it aside.

"Okay," she told Ace.

He took a step forward, releasing the tension on the rope. She freed the calf to its mother.

"Hey *matadora*," Sam said, running over to hug Jen.

"Thank goodness she didn't have horns," Jen said, laughing. "And you—"

"I know." Sam rolled her eyes and shook her head.

"Not that anyone would have noticed an orange-and-black cow with an upside-down brand."

"I'm so glad *you* noticed," Sam said.

"So glad that you're ready to take the afternoon off and play checkers with me?" Jen asked.

"Checkers?"

"I have a little car-trip checkerboard, but I never have company in the backseat." Jen pulled a pitiful frown. "Don't you feel sorry for me?"

"Not very, but I'm ready to rest the horses and take a nap, so I guess if you'll make lunch, we can play checkers afterward."

"Deal," Jen said, and the two friends shook hands.

There was a strange sound on the mountain that night. It wasn't the baying of hounds or the lonely howling of coyotes, and yet it was some kind of a cry.

Wakeful most of the night, Sam wanted to investigate, but she'd forced herself to wait until morning.

She'd had a lot of weird dreams between snatches of sleep.

In one, she'd been herself, but as a very little girl. Crouched down, curled into a kitten-tight ball, she'd played hide-and-seek. Holding her breath, trying not to giggle and give away her hiding spot, she'd suddenly realized she wanted to be found.

Struggling free of the dream and her hiding place in it, Sam knew she wasn't afraid of discovery. She was afraid no one would come looking for her.

It was weird, Sam thought, blinking awake. She wasn't lost and alone. She knew the way home and she was with Jen.

She gazed at the glowing numbers on her watch.

It was five o'clock. One disgruntled cow had continued her hooting moo until midnight. Then they'd been roused at about three by the new sound.

They'd fidgeted inside their sleeping bags, dozing, then waking, all that time.

"I hope it's not Pirate," Sam said as Jen rolled over in her sleeping bag to face her.

"Shh," Jen whispered. "If you wake that hooting cow, I'll strangle you. But that sound's not a horse. No way."

Sam sat up.

The sky had grayed in the east, she wasn't sleeping anyway, and she had time to investigate before they started the herd back to War Drum Flats.

"I'm going to see what it is," Sam said.

"You don't have to," Jen told her. "If it's something injured, you'll just feel bad."

"Yeah, but if I ignore it, I'll feel worse," Sam said.

"Well, take our first aid supplies," Jen said, yawning.

"I will." Sam pulled on her clothes and a jacket.

"Did we give the horses all the carrots? Whatever's up there isn't likely to be a carnivore."

"We've got plenty," Jen said, then gave a long sigh. "Just knowing you're going up there to tend to whatever it is makes me sleepy."

"Swell," Sam grumbled. "So if I disappear—"

"I'll send out a posse," Jen said, rolling on her side and pulling her sleeping bag up to cover her nose. "Unless you wake up that hooting cow. Then I won't be speaking to you, so what would be the point?"

Forty minutes into her ride, Sam realized the sound was human.

Fifteen minutes later, she recognized the voice begging for help.

"Okay Ace," Sam said, clucking the horse into a lope across the plateau. "This is what they call a moral dilemma."

"Won't anybody help me? I got a roll of hundred-dollar bills big enough to choke a mule and no one will help me!"

Well, that was progress, Sam thought. At least he realized his money wasn't doing him any good.

"Somebody! Anybody!" The voice cracked.

Ace's ears flicked toward the plea, but Sam didn't answer.

If Linc Slocum was trapped or injured, he'd better not have hurt Champ. Or Bub, Gator, or Shirley, for that matter. Even though the pack was a dangerous nuisance, she didn't blame the dogs.

Suddenly, Sam realized Slocum's voice was leading her to Cow Killer Caldera.

She shivered. If the terrain was too difficult for cattle, it might not be safe for Ace.

When she got close enough that she could make out Slocum's mumbling, she pulled rein and tied Ace to a sturdy aspen tree.

"No ground-tying this time, boy," she told the mustang. "Being left out here alone is one thing, but I will *not* take a chance on you leaving me here with him. No way."

Sam walked to the edge of the caldera. She wouldn't be able to tell Jen if it was really the remains of a volcano, but she could understand why Linc Slocum hadn't climbed out.

The sides were steep and sheer. The floor of the caldera must be five hundred feet lower than the top edge of what looked like a crater.

An experienced climber could probably make it out, but not Linc Slocum. Even though he looked small in the bottom of the crater, he wasn't in shape for the ascent.

There was no sign of Champ or the dogs, and Linc couldn't be hurt, at least not badly, because he was storming around with his hands on his hips, muttering. Suddenly, he saw her.

"Hey, you! Get me out of here!"

"Hi, Mr. Slocum," Sam said. "What'cha doing?"

Sam put a hand over her mouth to keep from

laughing. A nicer person probably wouldn't even think of laughing, but she loved his predicament.

"I'm trying to get out of here! That bacon-brained horse of mine acted like he'd never seen a dog before! They were just playin' and he dumped me right here, off the edge."

Sam had her own opinion about who was bacon-brained, but Slocum might be injured. If what he'd said was true, he'd fallen a long, long way to reach the bottom of this crater.

"Are you hurt?" she yelled.

"What?"

"Are. You. Hurt."

"No, but that Champ's going to be beggin'—"

Linc's sudden silence told her he'd remembered something. Everyone knew that when it came to horses, Sam Forster was notoriously softhearted.

As she watched, Slocum seemed to retrieve two things that might be his boots. Sam wondered how long it would take for Slocum to start offering a reward for his own rescue.

"Samantha, I'm gonna make you a deal," he said.

That was quick, Sam thought.

"I've got a nice, crisp hundred-dollar bill for you if you can rope me out of here."

Sam shook her head in disbelief.

"Mr. Slocum, my rope won't reach you. This crater is far too deep."

"Two hundred," he shouted up to her.

"I don't even believe this," Sam muttered to herself.

She almost reminded Linc of the last time he'd promised her a reward. He'd given her the money, all right, but not Hotspot's foal. She didn't remind him. He might think she was tempted, and she wasn't.

"Mr. Slocum, are you hungry?" she called instead.

"So hungry I could eat these boots!"

"Well, I don't think you'll have to do that. I'm going to throw you down a sack of carrots—"

"Carrots? Carrots!" he shrieked. "A man can't live on carrots!"

He was in no danger of starving to death before she brought back help. She waited for him to realize that.

"Okay, throw them down," he demanded.

She did.

"All right, Mr. Slocum, I'll try to get someone back to you before dark," Sam said.

"You can't leave me," he yelled.

"Well, I'm afraid I have to," she answered.

He mumbled something about her being a useless little monster, before shouting, "What would your father say?"

"I'm glad you asked, Mr. Slocum," Sam said, trying not to sound smug, "because my dad would say the ranch comes first. And, since I have a herd of cattle I need to bring to him by—" Sam looked at her watch. "Wow! Look at the time! I really do have to hurry."

"You can't leave me here alone," he moaned.

"I'll get you some help, Mr. Slocum. I promise."

And she would, Sam thought, walking back to Ace, but in the meantime, maybe Linc Slocum would think about what was really important.

Ace nuzzled her neck as she untied him, and then Sam swung into the saddle.

Revenge didn't have to be very harsh to be sweet.

Chapter Eighteen ∞

Under a pearl-gray sky full of heat, Sam and Jen navigated the path down to War Drum Flats.

"They're trying to play it cool," Sam whispered to Ace as she spotted Dad and Jed Kenworthy.

On this Father's Day morning, the two men sat their horses by the shallow lake. They pretended not to see their daughters escorting the herd down to meet them.

Jen rode three-quarters of the way up on the right side of the herd and Sam rode kitty-corner from her, three-quarters of the way back, on the left side. They couldn't talk this way, but it had proven the perfect way to keep the range cattle together.

So far, only two animals had caused problems: the

calfless Brangus and the black-and-orange calf they'd named Trouble.

After each of them had bolted from the herd, Sam and Jen had made a rule. If the Brangus wearing the Gold Dust brand bolted, Jen went after her while Sam and Ace held the herd. If Trouble skittered away, Sam, as the River Bend rider, would give chase.

They could have heard their dads now, if they'd spoken. They didn't, but Jeep neighed and Sundown, Jed's palomino, snorted a greeting.

Neither Ace nor Silly answered. Heads bobbing with each long stride, the horses kept up their watchful, flat-footed patrol alongside the herd.

"Just takin' care of business, aren't you, boy?" Sam asked Ace, rubbing his favorite spot at the base of his mane.

If we can just keep it together until we get down there, Dad will be proud, Sam thought.

The hard part was over. All they had to do was deliver the herd to their dads and tell them about Linc Slocum. Sam didn't know if she'd earned the right to be called a buckaroo.

When she saw Dad and Jed face each other and give slight nods of approval, she figured she was on her way.

In the movies, Dad and Jed would have ridden up galloping to greet them, but this was real life. Both men were cowboys. Short of a sudden storm, there was probably no faster way to start a stampede.

So they eased their horses toward their daughters. Any minute, Sam expected Dad and Jed to stop the herd so they could talk.

It didn't happen, and suddenly Sam realized the men were letting her and Jen decide whether to stop the herd or keep going.

"Wow," Jen muttered as she realized what Sam had.

"Yeah, wow," Sam replied quietly.

Her cheeks were sore from grinning by the time Jed reined his horse to a position opposite Jen, and Dad fell in across from her.

They'd ridden just a few yards more when Jen angled Silly in front of the crazy River Bend cow that had tried to butt her.

Sam narrowed her eyes toward Trouble. *Don't you dare make a break for it*, Sam thought toward the animal, but the Halloween-colored calf just tucked up close to her mother.

The herd stopped.

"Well," Jed said.

"Happy Father's Day," Jen and Sam said together, and then they laughed. Their chorus couldn't have come out better if they'd planned it.

"Brands appear to be on straight," Jed said, scanning the herd.

"Everybody's wearin' ear tags," Dad observed.

Jen and Sam met each other's eyes over the herd. Not everybody would recognize their dads' words for congratulations, but coming from cowboys, those few words were high praise.

"Everything went great," Jen said. "Nobody threw a shoe, or tagged their own ear, or got a brand upside down."

"Jen . . ."

"What's that?" Dad asked Sam.

"I didn't say anything. I was just laughing at my funny friend," Sam told him. "But one little thing went wrong."

Suddenly still, Dad waited.

"He's all right—"

"As all right as he ever is," Jen interrupted.

"—but Linc Slocum fell into Cow Killer Caldera."

It was Jed and Dad's turn to exchange looks.

"He did, did he?" Jed asked. "But you say he's okay?"

"Oh yeah," Sam told him. "He was complaining about the food I dropped to him."

Both men nodded.

"We'll get Sheriff Ballard out. He's pretty eager to test his new search-and-rescue horse," Dad said.

"Jinx!" Sam said to Jen. "Maybe you can see him in action. That will be so cool."

"I wonder how they'll get him out, though," Jen mused. "It might take a while to find someone who can rappel down and bring him back up."

"You say he's safe where he is, though?" Dad asked.

"He's fine, just cranky," Sam said.

"It's too bad we don't have a cell phone that would work from here," Jen said, frowning.

"Yep, it's a cryin' shame," Jed agreed, but the sarcasm in his voice said he didn't mind letting Slocum wait in the caldera just a little bit longer.

"Dad!" Jen said in an uncharacteristic squeak.

The sound made Dad and Sam laugh, but Trouble didn't find it a bit funny. The brindle calf sprinted past Jen, headed across the *playa*.

Without thinking, Sam sent Ace after the calf. White dust puffed in the calf's wake and its tiny hooves pecked marks in the alkali flat.

Everyone was watching and Sam knew she had to get this right. With the faintest touch, she guided Ace to the right.

Trouble must have glimpsed them from the corner of her eye, because she made a wide, sweeping turn away from Ace and headed back to her mother at a trot.

Sam followed at a distance, letting the calf lead the way. If Trouble swerved in either direction, she and Ace would block her.

Ace pranced proudly, aware of all eyes upon him. Sometimes, Sam thought, being watched wasn't so bad.

All at once, she flashed back to her early morning dream. And Linc.

He wasn't playing hide-and-seek, but no one had

come looking for him. She shivered. *He'd been out all night and no one had noticed.*

If anyone had, Jed would have known.

What about Rachel and Ryan? It was Father's Day, and neither of them had noticed their dad was missing.

Sam felt a twinge of guilt for thinking she needed revenge against Linc. She didn't. He'd brought plenty of misfortune on himself.

Suddenly, Trouble broke into a gallop.

"Crazy little girl," Sam said, but Ace matched the calf's speed and they were running, almost home free.

Sam's heart vaulted up. She could see the pride on Dad's face, even from here.

As Trouble rejoined her herd and Ace slid to a stop in a rush of white alkali powder, Dad rubbed the dust from one eye.

"You did fine, Sam," Dad said, clearing his throat. "Just fine."

Chapter Two ⋙

Sam turned to Ryan. Linc Slocum's son was as smooth and reserved as his father was lumpy and loud.

Dressed in a tan polo shirt and jeans, Ryan had sleek coffee-colored hair that he wore a little long. He looked European, rich, and, right now, relieved.

"Did Jennifer tell you what I had in mind?" Ryan asked.

"About the colts," Sam said.

"Ah." He sounded disappointed, but just for a second. Had he expected Jen to ask the favor for him? Apparently not, because Ryan's eyes brightened as he asked, "Would you like a look at him, then?"

Sam guessed her grin was answer enough, because Ryan moved to open the back of the trailer.

The seconds it took Ryan to work the trailer latch free cranked up Sam's eagerness until she wanted to jump in and help.

Would the colt be an Appaloosa like his sweet-tempered mother or a stocky, heavy-headed animal like his sire?

The thick-maned stallion had been named Diablo by his owner, Rosa Perez. That was Spanish for "devil," but Rosa had claimed the stallion was "mild as a dove" with her.

Two horses backed from the trailer as one. The mare curved around the foal with such tenderness, Sam could barely see him.

She had forgotten Apache Hotspot was so beautiful. The young mare showed the best of her Thoroughbred and Appaloosa heritage. Her cocoa-brown head, neck, mane, and front legs flowed into a snow-white body sprinkled with brown.

"Hotspot looks wonderful," Sam said, recalling what she'd heard of the foal's difficult birth and the mare's anxiety afterward. "But she sure doesn't want me to see—"

Sam broke off, hoping Ryan would supply the colt's name.

"Shy Boots," Ryan announced.

It suited him, Sam thought, as Hotspot danced restlessly aside.

Gangly and timid, the colt ducked his head, then peered up at Sam through impossibly long eyelashes.

"Ohhh." Sam felt an instant tug at her heart.

Cocoa-brown like his dam, Shy Boots had a perfect white blanket over his hips. It was marked with spatters that looked like chocolate snowflakes. Pure white stockings reached from his faintly striped hooves to his knees.

"Ryan, he's darling."

"He'd rather be called 'magnificent,'" Ryan said. "But I suppose that will come with time."

Sam laughed. Sophisticated Ryan was actually speaking for his horse. Sam did it all the time, but this was the first time she'd heard it from him.

A squeaking snort came from the barn corral. Sam turned to see Tempest pressing against the fence, watching Shy Boots.

"She wants to play with him," Sam said.

"Then we won't keep the lady waiting," Ryan said.

He led Hotspot toward the corral, and Sam opened the gate. Shy Boots stayed so close to his mother, their burnished coats seemed to merge.

Until he saw Tempest.

Then, the colt frisked a few brave steps away.

Dark Sunshine flattened her ears, warning the newcomers from across the pen.

"Dallas said we should keep hold of the mares, at least 'til we see how they do together," Sam said.

"Very well," Ryan said.

The foals wasted no time inspecting each other.

Black muzzle touched brown before two exploring nickers erupted. Tempest made loud snuffling noises as she sniffed the colt's face. Shy Boots flicked his ears back and rolled his eyes. Tempest's ears sagged to each side, showing the colt she meant no harm by her curiosity.

Both foals raised their heads. Each tried to reach higher, until Shy Boots reared and Tempest snapped her teeth at his front legs.

Sam glanced at Dark Sunshine, but the mare had fallen to grazing. That must mean she wasn't worried.

As they reached some equine agreement, both foals' tiny brush–like tails flicked up and they burst into a run. Circling the corral, Tempest chased Shy Boots, nipping at his tail. Shy Boots zigzagged past his mother, nearly rammed Dark Sunshine, then wheeled to confront Tempest. They were off again, this time with Tempest in retreat.

Their joy was contagious. Across the ranch yard, the saddle herd began galloping around the ten-acre pasture, too.

"Last year your dad said Hotspot's foal might be 'fast as a caged squirrel,'" Sam told Ryan.

"He does manage those long legs rather well." Ryan sounded like a parent trying to be modest.

Ryan looked so proud and so fond of Shy Boots,

she decided not to mention that Linc had also said she could have the foal.

Something in Shy Boots cut through Ryan's cold reserve and made him happy. She wouldn't think of holding Linc to his offer.

The foals returned to their mothers and nursed so briefly, it seemed they were checking in, rather than seeking meals.

Dark Sunshine rested her chin on Tempest's back. Hotspot grazed and Shy Boots imitated her, spreading his front legs wide as he tried to nibble the sparse grass.

"Is he eating solid food already?" Sam asked.

"Trying," Ryan said. "Each day he chews more and nurses less."

Dark Sunshine was more watchful of Tempest than Hotspot was of Shy Boots. As Sam and Ryan eased out of the pen, Sam saw Dallas and mentioned the difference between the two mares.

"That's the way of it," Dallas said. "While they're little, filly foals are closer to their mamas. Once they're yearlings, though, the moms show more attachment to the colts."

Sam mulled that over, trying to make sense of it. Since young mares and young stallions were both driven from the herds by their sires, what were the mares thinking?

Tired out, Shy Boots flung himself down for a nap beside his grazing mother. As his tiny brown head scrubbed back and forth in the grass, trying to find a comfortable position, Sam decided his delicate bone structure showed no sign of his hammerhead father.

Tempest watched her playmate doze, but when she turned to bite the area above her tail, scratching an itch, she did it loudly. Then she used a hind hoof to scratch behind her ear. Fighting for balance, Tempest squealed, then looked at Shy Boots to see if he'd noticed.

The colt's long eyelashes stayed closed.

"She's doing everything she can to get his attention," Sam said as Tempest bolted into another lap around the corral. "I wish he and Hotspot could stay."

"So do I." Ryan spoke up quickly, as if Sam's words were the go-ahead he'd needed. "That's what I intended to ask of you."

So this was why Jen had said she couldn't give Ryan the permission he needed. Sam swallowed hard. There was no way in the universe Dad would allow more horses at the ranch.

"Then, as I drove over here," Ryan went on, "I realized my father would find them at River Bend."

"Find them?" Sam asked.

Ryan drew a breath. His explanation was probably going to be a long one.

"A few days ago, my father had Hotspot trailered over to Sterling Stables to be bred to Cloud

Cap, a stallion of good bloodlines," Ryan began.

Sam nodded.

"Shy Boots went along, since he's still nursing," Ryan said. "And, according to everyone watching, that's why, when Cloud Cap was loosed to Hotspot, she attacked him. She thought she needed to protect Shy Boots from the stallion."

She might have been right, Sam thought. In mustang herds, stallions sometimes killed foals that weren't their own.

"When Mr. Sterling opened the gate, Cloud Cap didn't have to be coaxed away from Hotspot. He fled." Ryan's shoulders lifted in a slight shrug. "Mr. Sterling suggested a second try after Shy Boots was weaned. He was polite about it, saying it happened now and then, but when my father returned home, he condemned Boots as a mongrel that had ruined everything."

"You can't let him think that way," Sam warned Ryan. She'd seen Linc Slocum's cruelty. The Phantom wore a scar from it.

"I did my best," Ryan said. "I reminded him of Hotspot's bloodlines and Diablo's stamina. Eventually, he calmed down. He agreed—at least I thought he had—to merely wean Boots early."

"He's only a few weeks old," Sam protested.

"I know. I'm afraid he'll be perpetually timid." Ryan stared away from the corral, past River Bend's bridge. "Hotspot is his only family. Take him

away too young and he'll have no one but me."
Ryan gave a short, mocking laugh. "And I'm the
last one who could teach him what it means to be a
Western horse."

"Ryan . . ." Sam began, but Ryan motioned her
to wait.

"All the same, I agreed to early weaning, because
it seemed the safest route."

Safest? Sam didn't like the sound of that.

"This morning, I was supposed to take Hotspot
back to Sterling Stables without Boots."

Ryan cleared his throat, then he gripped both of
Sam's shoulders.

She would have twisted away if he hadn't looked
down into her eyes with desperation.

"This morning, before I left, my father was on
the telephone telling someone that the easiest way
to 'wean' Boots was to cull him."

"What did he mean by that?" Sam asked, but
her heart was already plummeting.

Linc Slocum had scarred the Phantom's neck and
caused much of the stallion's dislike for humans.
What would he do to a "mongrel" foal like Shy
Boots?

"He wants to have Boots destroyed."

Horror slashed through Sam's imagination. She
thought of bullets, syringes full of poison. . . . But
when her eyes settled on Shy Boots, she realized it
wouldn't take much to end his new life.

"Please," Ryan said, when Sam stayed silent. "Help me hide them where my father won't think to look. I wouldn't ask, Samantha, but you're my only hope."

AVON BOOKS
An Imprint of HarperCollins*Publishers*

www.harperchildrens.com   www.phantomstallion.com